Sosa Gang 2

Romell Tukes

Lock Down Publications and Ca$h
Presents
Sosa Gang 2
A Novel by *Romell Tukes*

Romell Tukes

Lock Down Publications
Po Box 944
Stockbridge, Ga 30281

Visit our website @
www.lockdownpublications.com

Copyright 2023 by Romell Tukes
Sosa Gang 2

First Edition February 2023
Printed in the United States of America

Lock Down Publications
Like our page on Facebook: Lock Down Publications @
www.facebook.com/lockdownpublications.ldp
Book interior design by: **Shawn Walker**
Edited by: **Mia Rucker**

Stay Connected with Us!

Text **LOCKDOWN** to 22828 to stay up-to-date with new releases, sneak peaks, contests and more...
Thank you.

Submission Guideline.

Submit the first three chapters of your completed manuscript to ldpsubmissions@gmail.com, subject line: Your book's title. The manuscript must be in a .doc file and sent as an attachment. Document should be in Times New Roman, double spaced and in size 12 font. Also, provide your synopsis and full contact information. If sending multiple submissions, they must each be in a separate email.

Have a story but no way to send it electronically? You can still submit to LDP/Ca$h Presents. Send in the first three chapters, written or typed, of your completed manuscript to:

LDP: Submissions Dept
Po Box 944
Stockbridge, Ga 30281

DO NOT send original manuscript. Must be a duplicate.

Provide your synopsis and a cover letter containing your full contact information.

Thanks for considering LDP and Ca$h Presents.

Acknowledgements

First and foremost all praises are due to Allah, shout to all the readers rocking with me. Shout to NYC my city Yonkers and Peeky (914) CB, Lingo, Frazier, Art, Tone Touch, Chino, Baby James, Bonger, YB, and Moreno. My BK team Tim Day, OG Chuck and LIl YB from DOD, big shout to Philly my guys Big C, Dame, Legs, Banger and OG Muchie. Much love to da south, the west and the mid-west y'all know da vybeez. Respect and love to all the queens out there and kings. I'm dropping street lit shit everytime I put my heart into it so you can relate. Hit me on Facebook @ "Bama Author": from NYC. Shut to Lockdown Publications and Ca$h the game is ours keep your eyes and ears open. Free all the good women and men in the cage stay free mentally keep a peace of mind Love yall.

Romell Tukes

PROLOGUE

PHILLY, PA
SIX MONTHS AGO ...

Sosa and his gang were at the top of the food chain in the city of brotherly love. Last few months after Sosa killed his brother Block for becoming a snitch, his life changed.

Barry, who is Sosa's pops, opened a lane for Sosa, giving his block position which was locking down the streets. Once Sosa got on, he put his gang on for others all over Philly. Twin, Sosa's right-hand man, was from south Philly and was a known shooter. Lil Hak was from southwest around Sosa's area. He had his crew of savages locking down his side of town. Lez repped west Philly where he was loved and built the gang ground up on the westside. The northside was run by Gee who was doing time, so the D.C. Crew had that side under their authority. Sosa was able to bring all these sides together and make things happen.

Sosa's gang rivals were a crew called Outlaws who were just as vicious as the gang and they were seeing big money. Crispy and Sin were the main hitters to the Outlaws but word on the streets was they were really the small fish in the ocean. The Outlaws had ranks and there were a few more people over them in the crew but that identity was a big secret.

One night the Outlaws crept up on Lil Hak while talking to the D.C. Crew and did a drive by, hitting someone from the D.C. Crew. Roddy and Wayne were the leaders of the D.C. Crew. Since Wayne was locked up, Roddy had been holding down the streets. Sosa's gang and the D.C. Crew teamed up and took over the streets, but when Roddy got hit up shit started to get real nasty.

Lil Hak ended up having a shooting with his ops with Sosa there and the police arrived on the scene and caught a headshot. Lil Hak was hiding out after killing a cop.

Barry owed a Hala store and he let a very dependable Muslim brother run it, but inside, Barry hid a lot of money and drugs. Only few people knew of this, so one morning Barry went there to check on his stash and everything was gone— tons of coke and over a million dollars. Barry knew something was wrong when the Muslim man up front told him the front door was open when he arrived that morning.

***

Kilow was a dirty cop trying to make his way into the drug game by robbing and killing other dealers. He even had a few trap spots in Delaware and on the outskirts of the city. One thing nobody knew was that Kilow was Lez's brother but they did not fuck with each other at all.

One night, Kilow was trying to extort a new drug dealer in North Philly named Max after Crispy and Sin was killed by the Sosa Gang. Kilow had no clue Max's big homie was the famous OG Kane who had just come home from a bid in the feds. OG Kane was one of the leaders of the Outlaws and he was out to take over the streets that he'd shed blood in growing up in the Philly jungle.

***

Foxy came up in west Philly. She was Lez's ex-girlfriend and an official street bitch. It wasn't until Twin killed her brother Dawgy that the real her came out of her soul. She formed a team of bad bitches to kill the Sosa Gang for her brother's death but it didn't go as planned. Every time she planned a hit, some shit always went wrong.

Foxy hoped she would never have to cross paths with her ex Lez while gunning for his homies. Foxy had a big secret she never told Lez because she knew about his beef with the Outlaws. The truth was Foxy's dad was one of the main leaders beside three more members and she was one of them. Foxy tried to live a regular life even though she had a high rank and a seat at the table within the Outlaws. Now her dad was out she knew the city would never be the same …

CHAPTER 1
CAMDEN, NJ

"Yo, Roy! Who the fuck is that cat, bro? I ain't about to just walk away and take a ten-thousand-dollar loss," a local hustler named Texas stated.

"Texas, chill, bro. It's only ten bandz you lost on the dice game. I know you got that times ten," Ray said in the middle of a crowd full of gamblers.

They were in McGuire Projects, the home of Ray and a bunch of gang members, but everybody was getting money. Now, Ray's cousin Lil Hak was in town getting big money.

Lil Hak paid Texas no mind as he continued to shoot dice on the wall on the side of one of the buildings.

"Fuck dat shit. I want my fucking money! That nigga just won thirty thousand, and he not even from around here, bro," Texas yelled as everybody was paying him close attention, knowing Texas was a hothead and he had a small body count already.

"Texas, you wilding, man." Ray tried to be cool with him because he knew Texas had been sipping Lean.

"Fuck you and that Philly nigga! This my hood! On blood," Texas shouted as the dice game stopped.

Bloc … Bloc …

Texas's head flew off his shoulders and blood landed on at least five people before the crowd went into chaos.

Lil Hak placed the murder weapon back in his lower back. He was going to let Texas keep talking but when he disrespected him and his cousin, he had to show niggas what that Philly gunplay was really hitting on. "We out," Lil Hak said, walking over Texas's dead body after collecting the money all over the floor.

"You can't be doing shit like that, cuz. Real talk. Niggas know me and where my mom live," Ray cried, regretting letting Lil Hak come out to his city to lay law and get to a bag.

Before Lil Hak came out to Camden which was 20 minutes or less away from north Philly, Ray was doing his thing. Lil Hak helped him elevate from selling ounces to whole keys, but drama came with that. Lil Hak had been hiding in Camden for six months now, on the run from killing a cop, but the case went unsolved and Lil Hak didn't know as of yet. Since being in Camden, Lil Hak killed three people. Ray knew and now people were starting to look at him funny.

"I got you, cuz, don't worry," Lil Hak says, climbing in the passenger's seat of Ray's Range Rover.

"Nigga, you finna get both of us killed out here." Ray complained but Lil Hak turned up the Polo G album, tuning him out.

Lil Hak was supposed to meet up with a few Sosa Gang niggas later to drop him off some product. Twice a month Sosa sent a van fill of work for Lil Hak so he can get to a bag on the run but Lil Hak was ready to come to Philly.

***

LONDON, U.K.

Sosa took a few days to come out to London for a trip away from Philly, the city he loved but hated at times. Karlee, his girlfriend, wanted to come out to go shopping and have a good time. She was out shopping now at a Dior outlet. They were staying at a magnificent beachfront villa. There was a golf course, two floors, and large master bedrooms and master bathrooms. Jetted tubs, three fireplaces, and a four-season sunroom to enjoy early morning quiet time.

Sosa was in the sunroom watching TV, sipping coffee, thinking about all the freaky shit he and Karlee did last night. He knew his trip may be short lived due to all the issues he had been having back home with his crew and the Outlaws.

Back when Sin and Crispy got murked, he thought that was the ending to the Outlaws but it seemed like their death only made them stronger. Now there were rumors of a man named OG Kane taking over the crew, trying to take control of the drug turfs in the city, but Sosa refused to let that happen.

The past few weeks, a lot of his soldiers had been coming up dead, but his people had also been firing at places the Outlaw niggas were. Lucky he had the help of the D.C. Crew but Roddy was in a wheelchair for life after being shot up by the Outlaws. Roddy's brother Wayne was supposed to start trial in a few days but his trial had been held off due to his lawyer's sickness.

Sosa's dad was back on his feet in no time after getting robbed. Sosa couldn't believe someone robbed his dad for all the shit he told him. Barry pressed Sosa at first, thinking he did it, but Sosa explained to his dad he was out of town that night with Twin for two days so that took him out that bracket. Life was supposed to be good for Sosa. He had money, cars, a new mansion, a girl, a crew eating, but he felt like things could get worst. His main focus right now was finding out who OG Kane was and what he had up his sleeve.

Twin was doing his research on the Kane nigga and all he was getting was that Kane had been away for a while and had some kids somewhere in the city. One thing Sosa knew for a fact was he was flooding the streets with good dope and coke because his crew had been telling him.

The spots where the Outlaw niggas were selling drugs, feins flooded the areas day and night at all hours. Sosa had good product but nothing was like what he had been hearing about. Lez told him feins were saying the Outlaws had that coke and dope them BMF niggas used to flood the streets with in the 1970's and 1980's. Sosa planned to speak to his dad about this so he could try to get some better product.

Romell Tukes

CHAPTER 2
NORRISTOWN, PA

Right outside of Philly was a rich, upscale area called Norristown where only the rich and wealthy people rested their heads. Today, that nice, quiet area was being staked out by a group of gangstas who went by the name Sosa Gang.

Twin lead the two-van duo parked back-to-back, watching the mansion owned by a man whose real name was Vince but most people called him Vee. Sosa Gang had been watching Vee for a few months now because the streets were talking and they were saying Vee is the one who had been putting hits out and money on the Sosa Gang's head, especially the top four. Everybody who was somebody knew the top four was Sosa, Twin, Lil Hak, and last but not least Lez. Vee's name wasn't the only person he had been hearing about. There was a man named OG Kane that had been ringing, but Kane was like a ghost.

Twin watched the mansion closely with four other young shooters ready to put in some work for the name and the gang. Twin had been chasing money and making sure his crew ate and grew. South Philly was a war zone right now because of these Vee and OG Kane characters he had been hearing about daily.

All of Twin's goon had earpieces in their ears which were walkie talkies. They all had on three level vests, M4 Carbina's, M16's some had with a collapsible butt stock, lemon squeeze action, long silencers, and night vision goggles.

"Everybody on point? Mic check," Twin says into the walkie talkie to get a response from everybody.

"Twin, the bedroom light just went off," Lil Jet said who was Zels' little cousin. When Zels got killed, that took a lot out of him, especially his sister Traina who is still truly in love with Zels.

"Ight. In five seconds, I want van number two, Team B, to make way into the back," Twin says, counting down from five.

The shooters quietly slid out the van and sneaked into the large back yard through a small gate. They crept on the side of the wall as if they were military trained to be a real assassin team.

Twin and his crew then made their way towards the front door with a bag of locksmith equipment that would be able to get them inside and disconnect the security alarm.

"It's working?" Twin asked Lil Jet who was working on the front door. If this ain't work, Twin hoped Team B would be able to let them inside once they were in.

"Got it," Lil Jet said, seeing the door slowly crack open, creating no noise as they plan to shock and discredit the enemy.

The home had a breathtaking view not only on the outside but on the inside it was lavish and classy.

"Team B, take downstairs and clear it while I go up," Twin said.

"Copy," the Team B said all in their correct positions.

The darkness of the house made a few of them doubtful as to where they were going but they followed the wall and avoided bumping into anything.

Twin had on night vision goggles as he clenched the smoke grenade he had in his cargo pants pocket just in case he wanted to clear a room out before entering.

There were loud snores coming from the room with the double doors to his right which made him freeze and place a finger up.

Twin crawled on the wall and slowly turned the loose doorknob to hear the snores louder. He saw an older man laying on his back with a young Spanish woman on her stomach with her fat ass in the air.

Vee popped up out his sleep like a real robot and fired a bullet from a Glock 45 striking one of Twin's men in the forehead.

Psst, Psst, Psst, Psst, Psst ...

Twin struck Vee in the chest and arm he was shooting from. Twin rushed Vee to take the gun from him, putting his weapon to his face as Vee fought for his life. The woman was dragged out the bed and pinned to the floor with a gun to her temple.

"Who had been putting money on Sosa Gang head?" Twin asked.

"Me." Vee's breaths were getting shorter and shorter as blood started to cover his chest and bed.

"Who else?" Twin asked in a demand.

"Outlaws."

"I know that, bitch nigga, but who?"

"OG Kane and…" Vee tried to get another name out but it didn't make it. Vee's eyes rolled behind his head. Twin saw he was done. He thought about asking the woman, but she hadn't said a word of English since she had been crying because she was Vee's maid from Mexico. "Kill her," Twin said as his men did as he asked.

Twin and Lil Jet frozen on the way out, briefly in sorrow as they witnessed their soldier laying dead in front of them. The kid killed was Lil Jet's best friend.

CHAPTER 3
NEW YORK CITY, NY

Foxy came out to New York to do some shopping for the first time here. She had on a Gucci dress and sunglasses, looking like the true boss bitch she really stood for. Three of her girls came out to have fun on their free shopping spree that was on their girl Foxy. She had been in New York for two days, already blowing $150,000 on her and the girls.

The past year had been a big headache for Foxy, dealing with her brother Dawgy's death and other family issues. When she received the news about Sosa Gang being responsibile for her brother's death, she couldn't believe it. Her ex-boyfriend and first lover Lez was down with Sosa Gang and he used to bring her around the gang. She had a sit down with Lez and asked him if he was the one who did it. Lez denied killing her brother because he honestly didn't, and he expressed that to her. Deep down he could tell she ain't wanna hear that shit. Foxy told Lez if she found out he had anything to do with her brother's death then they would have an issue. Truth was Foxy still loved him but from a distance because she couldn't trust him. That was one reason for their breakup.

There was one big secret Foxy had been holding back from Lez and everybody, but she felt like it was time to bright it to light. Wintertime was over so she knew it was about to be a crazy spring in the city once she showed her true identity.

Foxy was always an active leader member of the Outlaws but she was just low key and distant. There were many days when she wanted to pillow talk with Lez when they were a couple and tell him who she really was. When she used to hear about the beef with Sosa Gang and the Outlaws, all she had to do was snap her fingers and she could've defused it all in a matter of seconds.

Growing up, while her father was in prison, he gave her a position in the Outlaws. There were only four seats at the top rank and Foxy had one of them. The only way out them seats once you're voted in is death. Foxy understood that growing up so she focused on living a regular life and letting niggas like Sin and Crispy be the face to the group.

Foxy's dad, OG Kane, was home from jail and he wanted to take control of the city which would be hard because Sosa Gang and the D.C. Crew had mostly shit sewed up. Showing face would shock a lot of people but she was more than ready. Foxy had her own crew of female shooters ready to kill for her and they were bad bitches.

Having her father home felt like he was still gone because they still didn't have any type of father and daughter relationship. Foxy was supposed to meet with her dad in a few days for their meeting. This would be her first time seeing him since he had been home. Today, her and her girls planned to hit up the city and turn up before sliding back out to Philly.

***

DOWNTOWN, PHILLY

OG Kane enjoyed his meal at Fogo De Choo as two security guards posted up near the front entrance, watching the door for his safety. He sat there thinking about the crazy news he heard about Vee and how he got murdered in his own home days ago. Kane had it in his mind who took his best friend's life. The Sosa Gang. There would be a lot of blood spilled over Vee's death; no question in his mind.

He and Vee go way back since little kids in the park, running around with dirty clothes. When Kane went to prison for over twenty years, Vee was one of the few people that was there for him and was very helpful and supportive. Vee owned two barbershops by the time Kane came home, but then Vee started fucking with Kane and he ended up getting caught in the cross fire.

While in jail, Kane was hearing about these Sosa Gang niggas, how the young bulls had the city in a chokehold, but now that he was home, he planned to show them how the real OG's do.

Growing up in his era, the original Black Mafia, which was Philly's most legendary crime family, showed him how to hustle, kill, move, talk, and carry himself. OG Kane learned a lot from the real OG's. Now he was teaching other young men like Max. Kane killed Officer Kilow because he knew eventually he would become a problem.

Since he had been home, he had his crew flooding the streets with dope and coke. They were also recruiting any and everybody willing to kill and get money. Kane was giving out $10,000 advances for soldiers to join the gang and people were coming left and right. He planned to have a sit down with his daughter soon to speak to her. Kane had tough love for his daughter because he didn't know how to give love. He was cold-hearted but he still loved her. He never loved another woman besides Foxy and his wife. His daughter was still a part of the Outlaws, so he had to treat her like the boss she was.

CHAPTER 4
WEST, PHILLY

Lez watched his hood do big numbers early in the morning in a neighborhood called Da Bottom. Feins were flooding the streets to get there morning hits. Lez posted up across the street, leaning on a black Porsche Panamera Turbo S worth $190,000 fresh off the car lot.

With Sosa Gang and the D.C. Crew on the same blocks together getting money made him realize that with time, shit can change. The less beef in the street, the more crews can eat, but in Philly he knew it was every crew for themself. What he saw today made it clear that different crews can get money with the right leadership.

He remembered when he used to run these crazy streets in west Philly from Da Bottom to Overbrook and Wynnefield as a kid, he had big dreams of becoming rich and famous. Rich became a life-style, but he knew outside of Philly he was nobody; just a regular nigga trying to make ends meet. Lez had been focused on getting money on his side of town, but in north, south, and southwest the gang was in a crazy war. When they killed Crispy, they assumed it was the end of their beef with the Outlaws, but now it seemed never-ending. The news of Sin shocked the crew because it wasn't Sosa Gang or the D.C. Crew who did it, so that left a lot of people in a mystery limbo.

Hearing Foxy was sending chicks at his crew kinda fuck his head up because he never saw her on that type of time since knowing her, so he was a little surprised. It wasn't hard for him to figure out that Foxy came to the conclusion that his crew is the one who killed Dawgy, her brother. That wasn't the only thing on Lez's mind for the last couple of months. Losing his blood brother Kilow touched his heart. Even though he knew Kilow was a piece of shit regardless he was still his brother. Losing a brother and not knowing who the killer was hurt him more. Till this day he never told his crew Kilow was his brother because he knew they would look at him different, like he would rat before a normal street nigga would just because he had family in the force.

Lez saw a familiar face walking down the block. It was Mrs. Jamie, his childhood babysitter who helped raise him and Kilow. "Mrs. Jamie?" Lez said as she was about to step foot off the curb to go inside the crack house. Lez saw how bad Mrs. Jamie looked and he couldn't believe it. She looked dirty and old. Lez saw drugs take a toll on people, but the way Mrs. Jamie looked, he knew drugs fucked her up.

"Lez, is that you, baby?" Mrs. Jamie says, turning around.

"Hey, Mrs. Jamie. What you doing out here?"

"Oh, going for my morning walk." She lied, unable to look him in his eyes.

"Come on, Mrs. Jamie. I know you get high. This is me you talking to. I love you regardless."

"Shit, who am I kidding? Baby, I gotta get right. Ain't nothing like a wake and bake," she says with no shame.

"I know, but how's life."

"I'm okay, baby. This a nice car you have here. I hear you doing good for yourself out here." She licked her crusted, chapped lips.

"I'm maintaining."

"I'm sorry to hear about Kilow. He was a real good kid. He used to see me all the time and let me slide with a lot. He even caught me sucking two guys' dicks in that park." Mrs. Jamie pointed to the park next to them.

"I didn't want to hear all that." Lez laughed at how crazy she was.

"I can't believe OG Kane killed him. Well, I know him as Kane. I used to babysit him as well. Boy, he was a handful, I tell you."

"Hold on. How do you know he killed my brother?" Lez couldn't believe what he just heard.

"Oh, a few of my get-high buddies saw him do it one night. We be all over Philly. But, look, I have to go. My girl waiting on me." Mrs. Jamie saw a fat woman wave her down to join her so they could get high with the drugs she'd just coped.

Lez believed every word she told him just now because she never lied to him. The name OG Kane he had been hearing about a lot in the city lately, but now Kane had just made it to a bridge that he might not make it across.

***

NORTH, PHILLY

Gee was fresh home in his old hood, Nicetown, ran by Gee, but the only issue was everybody down there was now Sosa Gang. Since he heard Twin killed his sister, he fell back from the gang. He had been working a bullshit construction job to keep parole off his ass so he wouldn't go back to jail. Being home from prison felt good. He never wanted to go unless it was for real serious life or death type shit. The hardest part for him was coming home to start over brand new, from the ground up.

He had been hearing the Sosa Gang and the D.C. Crew names heavy in the streets. Gee had no clue how they came together but neither did he give a fuck. Gee wanted blood for his sister's death, and somebody was gonna pay regardless. First, he needed to stack some money and build his own crew to go against the deepest crew in the city.

When he came home, he started fucking with his ex-girlfriend Latifah who was a born Muslim from around his way and she was bad. Latifah wanted him to get back on his deen and worship Allah because Gee was a Muslim too, but he had been slacking on his duties as a Muslim man.

Luckily, he lived with his aunty who was always at work in the hospital, sometimes working a double. Gee planned to move in with Latifah who was in a hood called Badlands which was known for its drugs and murders thanks to the Outlaws who ran the area. Gee had a car already and a bank account with some money saved up, so he was still ahead of a bunch of niggas out there.

He prepared to get ready for work so he could drive to the construction site. The job was easy and he was making money, but every time he saw a Sosa Gang nigga, he wanted to shoot them, but he had to control himself. The main nigga he was looking for was Twin and he knew one day soon he would run into him.

CHAPTER 5
PHILLY COUNTY JAIL

Wayne was being released this morning after beating two murder charges yesterday in court. Everything got acquitted. He had been fighting the two charges for close to two years in the county jail. Wayne is the leader of the D.C. Crew, but while he was in jail, he let his brother run the show which he regretted now because his little brother Roddy was in the hospital paralyzed from the waist down.

In the jail cell, all he could think about was how the Outlaw niggas did his little brother and he wanted blood. Coming home off two murders to touch down on bullshit wasn't a smart thing, but he followed the G-code, which was the street code.

Waiting in the bullpen he couldn't wait to hit the outside of the wall to get back to his regular lifestyle which was only regular to him. To most it was dangerous. Since being locked up Wayne couldn't stop hearing about the Sosa Gang niggas who was taking over Philly. When he heard his crew and Sosa Gang teamed up, at first he was a little upset but he got over it. He had been meeting a lot of Sosa Gang niggas coming in and out of jail— some on shooting, drugs, money, robbery's and a few murders.

One member of the crew he disliked for a long time and that was Lez. The two of them had beef over a chick which led to a few shootouts in the hood. Wayne knew that was in the past, but he still was salty about that because not too many niggas can say they got into a shootout with Wayne and lived to talk about it.

"You that Wayne cat from the D.C. Crew who beat all those bodies?" a tall young skinny kid asked, sitting across the bullpen from him.

"You that rat nigga who telling on that Dominican kid who was supplying you from Uptown right?" Wayne responded, looking back at him to see that he put his head down.

"It's not what you think. I got a newborn, and my mom is dying of cancer," the kid told Wayne in a sad voice.

"Nigga, fuck your newborn and your mom, snitch nigga. Now don't say another word to me before I knock you the fuck out in here, cuz." Wayne got upset he even entertained the kid's conversation in the first place.

"Wayne, it's time get outta here, and don't kill nobody out there," a male CO said who knew Wyane very well. He used to bring him in food and drugs.

"Whatever. Let me out this mouse trap," Wayne said, getting up to leave.

After he got his property and items he was escorted to the front door. As soon as he walked out, he saw his girlfriend Abby, a beautiful, slim, dark-skinned woman who was 100% African and sexy. Abby's family were all descendants from African. Even she was born in West Africa. Abby knew Wayne forever. They had been a couple close to ten years now and she was a real trooper. When he was fighting his murder cases, she was right there by his side the whole way, no half-assing.

"Babe!" Abby yelled when seeing Wayne as she rushed into her man's arms like she hadn't seen him in years.

"I missed you." He smiled

"Nigga, please. I just saw you on Sunday," she replied, kissing his lips.

"Today is a new day," he said.

"Facts. Let's get away from here, please. I'm sick of looking at this jail."

"Shit, you!" Wayne walked to her Audi which was a push-to-start.

"You wanna go shopping?" She asked knowing he would want to change his jail clothes into some fly designer shit.

"First, I wanna go see my brother. Then, we can go to the KOP Mall."

"The King of Prussia mall?" She asked to make sure that's what he meant.

"Yeah, but first, take me to the hospital."

"Gotchu," she said, knowing he was going to be hurt to see his brother in his new fucked up condition.

***

TEMPLE HOSPITAL, PHILLY

The ride to the hospital was short because they were laughing and talking, but Wayne wanted to go inside by himself.

"Can you wait here for me, babe?" Wayne asked Abby, hoping she understood.

"Sure," she said

"Thanks. I love you."

"Love you, too," she told him back, watching him walk into the hospital with his head down. She remembered the day she told him Roddy got shot up. She heard his tears over the phone. Abby knew Roddy was all Wayne had growing up and the two were close, so she felt his pain but at least he was alive. She lost her brother a few years back to a robbery, so she knew the pain could be worst.

"Where can I find the patients that come outta comas?" Wayne asked a doctor who was about to walk past him in a rush because today was a busy day.

"On the third floor. Are you looking for somebody?" The doctor asked, finally lifting his head.

"Yes. Roddy Williams."

"Oh, yes. Roddy's doing better," the doctor said, knowing who Roddy was because he saved his life some months ago.

"You know him?"

"Yes. He's my patient. We're hoping to have him up and out in a few weeks," the doctor said with a smile.

"So, he'll be able to walk?"

"No. Never again. But he can use his upper body now, unlike a few months ago. He couldn't do shit."

"Thanks."

"Sure, anytime. He's in room three-twenty-one, sir," the doctor shouted before walking off.

Wayne made his way to the third floor, happy his brother was alive. The third floor smelled like piss, shit, and diapers mixed all into one. He entered the room to see his little brother playing a XBOX in the hospital bed. Nobody knew Wayne was coming home so he knew this would be a big surprise to his brother. "So, this is what you on now?" Wayne asked as he saw Roddy's shocked look.

"What the fuck? Ohhh, shit!" Roddy shouted in happiness. His legs couldn't move but his upper body did.

"I beat the cases, bro. It's litty. I'm out here now." Wayne saw his brother's lower body and almost cried but he knew he had to focus.

"That's the creed of Allah," Roddy said, seeing his brother stare at his legs.

"Facts."

"Abby had been coming to see me and shit."

"She told me." Wayne took a seat next to his brother's bed.

"I can't believe this shit, bro. I'm fucked up for life now." Roddy's voices saddened.

"You gonna be good, bro. Facts."

"I fucking hate them Outlaw niggas. I was happy when I saw them on the news," Roddy said.

"That was only the beginning. When I was in jail, my man said a nigga name OG Kane running the show now, so I'ma get to the bottom of it. Trust me," Wayne stated.

"I want you to lay low, bro. You fresh home." Roddy knew how his brother got down and he could turn the city up overnight.

"It's not chill time until all dem niggas wiped out, bro."

"If you gonna really do this shit, do it with Sosa Gang at least."

"I'ma fuck with them on the money tip but we don't need nobody to handle our war, 'cause them niggas put my brother in a wheelchair."

"I'ma be alright. Just hold down the fam and the crew, bro."

"That's all I knew, cuz." Wayne already knew what needed to be done.

The brothers kicked it for over an hour, then Wayne went to Abby's crib and fucked her all night long.

CHAPTER 6
WEST, PHILLY

Lez cruised into the Wynnefield section of west Philly he controlled, but for the past couple of weeks he had been hearing about a kid named Eaze-T who had been getting big money in Wynnefield.

"Pull into that lot. We can go up the block on foot and peek into the building across the street from where they trapping at," Lil Brad stated in the passenger's seat of the stolen car.

"How old are you?" Lez asked.

"Eighteen."

"How many drills you had been on?"

"A few," Lil Brad shot back.

"What's a few, bro?"

"I slid on niggas twice, bro. I know what to do," Lil Brand said making Lez laugh as he parked the car.

"Just sit back, young bull, and watch the play." Lez hopped out the parked car with a black ski mask and a FN handgun tucked under his shirt.

Lil Brad was new to the gang. Lez saw something in him that made him want to keep him around. Lez was from the same building as Lil Brad. He knew the young man's parents who both were doing over 100 years in prison. Since he lost his parents to the system, Lil Brad's grand mom raised him. Lez saw a lot of him in the young man, so he took him under his wing and put him down on some money.

Lil Brad hopped out and followed the man he looked up to since he was a kid.

***

"We run this shit now, cuz. Look at all this money we can make in one day," Eaze-T said, pulling out a wad of money, all blue and pink faces.

Eaze-T was really from northeast Philly around Oxford Circle, but when his brother Rizzy told him about how he could get some money on his side of town, he was opening up shop and he was down. Four of his goons stood around waiting on feins to come through the block so they could get to a bag. Being a part of one of the most dangerous crews in the city made him feel empowered and like a real nigga.

"We gotta go count this money and grab some more shit, unless y'all got more shit left?" Eaze-T asked his goons he brought with him from his good Oxford Circle.

"Nah," a fat nigga said.

"We all out," Eaze-T's best friend Baby E stated looking at the guys.

"Let's go upstairs real quick," Eaze-T said walking up the stairs.

Inside the dirty brick apartment building they went to a unit on the second floor. Stepping into the crib they saw a black, skinny, ashy nigga smoking crack out a glass pipe with a burnt tip.

"Damn, nigga, go in the back and smoke that stanky shit," Eaze-T shouted as the crackhead jumped up and rushed to the back, wearing only a pair of underwear.

The crew all covered their mouths, trying not to catch a contact from the smell.

Eaze-T went in the closet and got the rest of the drugs he had left, which was only a half a key bagged up into ounces and grams. "This is all we have left," Eaze-T said before 2 gunmen ran in the apartment with guns out aimed at them.

"Don't move," Lez said, but Baby E jumped to get away.

Bloc ... Bloc ... Bloc ...

Brad shot Baby E in his face, killing him. The rest of them got nervous, now stuck.

"Take everything. We don't want no problems," Eaze-T said

"Who you work for?" Lez asked, seeing Eaze-T was hesitate to say.

Boom! Boom!

Lez shot one of Eaze-T's friends in the neck then looked at him.

"My brother Rizzy. He work for Kane. We all Outlaws," Eaze-T said, knowing these must be the vicious Sosa Gang niggas or the D.C. Crew niggas Rizzy told him to look out for because it was beef.

"What else can you tell me? I need to find them."

"I gave you who I work for, but I'm no snitch. Them my family."

"You sure?" Lil Brad added.

"Yeah," Eaze-T said, seeing Lez give Lil Brad a head nod and he killed his other friend before emptying the Glock on Eaze-T.

The crackhead walked out the backroom to see what was going on and he saw the dead bodies and gun. He went right back in the room to mind his business and finish getting high.

***

UPTOWN, PHILLY
NEXT DAY

Rizzy spent all night trying to comfort his mom because she was fucked up over his little brother's death. When she called him and told him about Eaze-T's death, he didn't want to believe it at first. He regretted bringing his little brother out to west Philly knowing they had beef in the town with Sosa Gang going on. This made war. To Rizzy, now it was very personal with him and Sosa Gang; his ops. Being down with the Outlaws meant any day you can become a victim to the streets just because of who you were down with.

Rizzy had always had been down with the Outlaws since he was 16 years old and he was now 24. Rizzy was getting money in York, PA where he was living with his aunty because his mom kicked him out of her house when she heard he was running with Sin. Rizzy and Sin where close friends growing up, but when he moved to York they got a little distant from each other. Hearing someone bodied his boy crushed him, but Rizzy knew how the Philly streets were. Coming back to Philly a few months ago, he linked up with his cousin Max and focused on this paper.

Tonight, he, Max, and Kane were meeting up to go over business deals and the Sosa Gang niggas. Rizzy knew there were three more other leaders who sat at the round table with Kane, but he knew it was a secret until the big meeting coming up in a few months.

It was 9:30PM when he pulled into the meeting's location which was in the back of a flower shop on a Main Street. Rizzy exited his car and walked into the cold shop to see an old lady cutting stems of pink roses.

"Everybody in the back, young man," the woman stated without even booking at him.

"Thank you." He walked to the back to smell cigar smoke. Walking through the door he saw Max and Kane waiting on him at a round table.

"My regards go out to your little brother, Rizzy. Have a seat so we can get this started," Kane said

"Good looks. Max, what's good, bro." Rizzy sat

"I'm iight, cuz. How you holding up?" Max asked

"Peachy," Rizzy says.

"I got a few small leads on our guys. Since they killed Vee, they had been moving sloppy, but we gonna mastermind. So, plot to get them soon because if we don't, they will fuck up our plans," Kane said

"They fucking with them D.C. Crew niggas and I hear Wayne home from beating them bodies," Max says.

"You sure? I ain't hear that?" Kane asked knowing how Wayne got down.

"Facts. I heard the same thing," Rizzy stated.

"Fuck him. Right now, we need to focus on these Sosa Gang niggas. We gonna start from the bottom up, but this shit gonna get ugly. I want y'all to kill all them niggas," Max said, knowing a lot of shooters ready to die for him. "What's up with the product and blocks?"

"We still hustle and take over blocks. I want soldiers all over the city. Rizzy, bring your people from York out here to help," Kane said.

"Ight, cool," Rizzy said.

"Next month we will meet again. Stay focused and positive, but be safe. Stay loaded. We Outlaws. We don't respect shit," Kane said before ending the meeting.

CHAPTER 7
DOWNTOWN, PHILLY

Today, Barry had a busy day, so he was up and out early in his white Rolls Royce Cullian SUV Limited Edition. He was dressed in a very clean, expensive black tailormade suit for his two important meetings. Barry's first meeting was with his lawyer, Mr. Luiscino, he had been having on his team for years, and he made the lawyer a rich man. Anybody close to Barry that ever ran into any legal problems he sent Luiscino and they were good.

Sosa had been handling all the drug affairs except dealing with the plug. Barry never gave up his real plug to nobody and he had no plans to. Barry couldn't believe the amount of bricks his son was moving. It was appealing to him. Even when his other son Block was alive, it would take him two weeks to move the same amount of keys Sosa could move in two days.

Having his own son killed was both hurtful and joyful because it hurt to have his own son killed, but he hated rats, and that was Block's death wish. Putting Sosa and his crew on to a bag was the best thing that ever happened to him because he was checking in so much money.

The five-star restaurant was barely empty this morning for his weekend brunch with his lawyer. Later, he had another meeting with a big-time investment company. Barry was bringing his beautiful girlfriend along because it was a double date meeting. Walking inside after parking in the front, he saw a bunch of white people, but that was the type of environment he chose to be in. Being around a bunch of hoodlums wasn't something he was into. It brought too much heat.

Mr. Luiscino was seated in the middle of the restaurant eating a large plate of food, but he had two more plates on the way. Mr. Luiscino weighed over three hundred pounds, but he was one of the biggest lawyers in the city of Philly. He did a lot of cases for the Mafia back in the days which brought his name to light. "Barry, you look younger. You have to give me your secret," Mr. Luiscino said, seeing his most loyal client arrive.

"Stay black," Barry said.

"That won't happen on the outside, but on the inside, I'm blacker than you."

"I bet, but I see you ordered already," Barry said sitting down.

"I was starving, I tell you," Mr. Luiscino said in his Italian accent.

"That's nothing new."

"I'm glad you here because I have something to tell you."

"Talk." Barry hoped it was good news.

"There is a new DEA lady in office, and she is blood-sucking thirsty, but a hot piece of ass, I tell you," Mr. Luiscino says.

"Okay. What does she have to do with me?" Barry said, playing dumb. Barry never told Luiscino he sold drugs. He came off as a businessman but he knew his lawyer read between the lines years ago. Every time he paid the lawyer to bail out drug dealers and fight cases dealing with murders and drug crimes, he knew sooner or later the lawyer would piece it all together.

"I'm just saying she is on some bullshit, but she's really only focused on these two crews that call themselves Sosa Gang and the Outlaws. Sad black men waste their life in the streets," Mr. Luiscino said as more food arrived.

Barry's head started to spin because he knew his son could be in serious shit, but the lawyer didn't know Barry had any ties to either crew, and if he did, he would most likely sell him out to the DEA for the right price. "What's her name?"

"Janasia."

"Okay. I'ma take care of your payment soon. So, how's work?" Barry asked, thinking about Sosa and meeting up with him.

"Same shit, but I got a meeting with the mayor. I'ma call you later," Mr. Lusicino says, finishing his meal.

Barry left, calling his son to get down to the bottom of this because he didn't need heat on him from no stupid street shit.

***

WEST, PHILLY

Foxy brought out her hot pink Audi R8 Spyder V10 coupe with her top down to enjoy the beautiful day. Since coming back from vacation, the only thing she had been focused on was recruiting all females to take over the west Philly streets with drugs, hookers, and she planned to open a few businesses to give back. She already had two ride or die bitches down with Beth and Rika from the projects who were sisters. The only thing in her way was Sosa Gang and the D.C. Crew who she had been seeing too much of on this side of town.

Looking around Overbrook she saw there was a lot of money to be made as dope feins waited on corners to be serviced. She had a small plan she put together while in New York. Foxy really wanted to get at Twin, but every time she would send a missile, it would fail of course. The streets had been talking about Lil Jet so she wanted to see if her girls could get at him to get at Twin.

Her dad had been calling her but she had been too busy to pick up and she was still upset at him for missing her whole life, but she didn't show it.

Foxy saw the two chicks outside with a few other girls looking like hood boogers with cute faces and fat asses. Beth and Rika rushed Foxy's fly ass car like she was a superstar while other chicks watched from a distance.

"Hey, girl. Where you had been at?" Rika, the dark skinned one, asked. She was medium height with a fat ass.

"I was in New York." Foxy hopped out in a skirt with Tammy Choo's on her feet. She had manicured with a fresh tatt on her right foot of a snake eating an apple.

"You making power moves," Beth said, looking at Foxy's attire, wondering how much everything cost her. Beth was the cute one besides a little acne on her face from time to time. She was slim but thick, brown skin, hazel eyes, dimples, and a nice smile.

"True dat, but I'm here for a reason. I need to speak to y'all," Foxy said, looking at the sisters.

"We listenin'," Rika says.

"You remember I told y'all soon it would be time to lock shit down?"

"Yeah. How could we forget?" Beth replied, never forgetting her girl's words the last time she talked to her.

"Well, it's time to get money. But, first, I need one of you to bag a little nigga named Lil Jet and put him under the wing until I figure out what to do with him," Foxy stated.

"Easy. I got that," Beth said smiling.

"I'ma swing back through today to give y'all the rundown on everything," Foxy told them.

"Cool," Rika says, holding back her happiness because her and her sister wer dead broke in the hood. They wanted a better life at only 19 years old.

CHAPTER 8
SOUTH, PHILLY

Max's cousin Fetty G counted a stack of money, leaning on a Maserati with a fake Rolex watch on his wrist.

"Yo, Fetty. We need some more work. Raq and me out." Two young hustlers approached Fetty, their boss, because they were selling $10 to $40 packs of crack and dog food.

"Run to the corner and tell the bull HB and Hoco to give y'all the rest of what's in the stash," Fetty G said, feeling like a boss.

"Iight."

Fetty G was from 17th and Wharton. He loved his hood, but it was dangerous. He smelled blood every night growing up on 17th. Growing up around mostly Sosa Gang niggas, he became one of them until his cousin Max became his plug and he started fucking with the Outlaws which was now heavy in numbers in the city.

Counting the hundred stacks, he saw his phone ring and it was his dad calling who was a dope fein. His block was beefing with a nigga name Kaba from 20th and Tasker. He was down with the D.C. Crew. Turning around he was blindsided by a pistol knocking his frail frame to the floor. "Ahhhhhh, fuck!" Fetty G looked up to see Lez and Kaba standing over him.

"You thought shit couldn't happen, though, bull," Kaba stated, firing his FN handgun that was so loud a row of cars' alarm systems went off.

BOOM! BOOM!

Fetty G's nose and a piece of his cheek flew off the deceased man's face.

Lez and Kaba had a car parked up on the corner waiting for them as the getaway car.

"Take us to 19th and Sigel," Kaba told the driver.

"Put your crew on his block. That shit yours now," Lez told Kaba, handing him three large store bags full of keys.

Kaba got his drugs from Sosa and the crew and he normally split everything with his D.C. Crew so niggas could eat. "Thank you, big bro." Kaba saw it was twenty keys in each bag.

"That's how we go, bro. Facts. We stronger as one," Lez stated.

"I don't know if you heard or not but Wayne home. I had been waiting on him to get at me, bro," Kaba stated.

"I heard," Lez said flatly, not showing too much of nothing.

"I know y'all history, bull, and y'all need to put that shit aside. The city need us," Kaba said because he really liked Lez and all the Sosa Gang leaders. They were solid.

"We good."

"Everybody knows y'all not. but good looking for today. It was perfect timing," Kaba said as the car pulled behind a Porsche Panamera that belonged to Lez.

"It's about a check now, bull. That's old beef. It's time to focus on what matters, young bull," Lez said, climbing out the getaway.

"I'ma get at you in a few days," Kaba shouted out the window before he and his driver pulled off.

Lez got in his Porsche thinking about Wayne being home and how odd it was about to be to ride for a nigga who he used to beef with in the streets. Since he was in south Philly he figured he'd slid over to Twin's trap to see if he was in the hood, but most likely he was because he was a block baby.

***

TEMPLE HOSPITAL, PHILLY

Wayne was leaving the hospital from checking on his brother who was still in the same condition as he left the first time. Seeing Roddy fucked up like that did something to him. The past few weeks he had been chilling with his wifey Abby, catching up on sex and family members with her and building. Roddy convinced him to have a sit down with Sosa today to go over business and talk about the dealings with his crew and Sosa Gang.

He recently coped a new red BMW 8 series coupe. So, he was on his way to meet Sosa uptown at a park to speak with him, but he wasn't ready to meet up with Lez. It took five minutes to get to the park he used to come to as a child which made him think about his mom who lost her life some years back to a sickness. Beating his murder cases and coming home felt unbelievable. He never in a million years would think he would be a free man. Talking to so many people in the jail doing life sentences about to get to ship to their prisons opened his eyes.

Wayne saw a nigga dressed in all black by the small lake, throwing rocks into the water. He figured it was Sosa, so he got out the car and walked over to him. "Sosa, I ain't seen you since you was a little nigga. And then I had no clue you was the Sosa, kid," Wayne said embracing Sosa.

"I like to keep a low profile, but that shit had been over with for the last few months. Welcome home. This is for you, bro, and please don't decline my gift. It comes with no agendas." Sosa handed Wayne a box.

"What's this?"

"Open it," Sosa said, seeing the man's eyes when he saw the bust down Patek Philippe diamond dial and bezel watch Sosa paid $120,000 for last week.

"Damn." Wayne placed the watch on his wrist, liking the fit.

"Something light, but thanks for coming out, and I send my regards to your brother. I go check on him daily. He family," Sosa stated seriously.

"I heard you go visit him. That's real."

"We haven't always seen eye to eye, especially you and Lez, but us coming together was the best thing that ever happened in the city," Sosa says.

"I agree, but I'ma keep it real. If I was home, this most likely wouldn't have happened because we stand on our own," Wayne said.

"So do we, but it's not about that pride shit. It's about making money and feeding the family, then everything else comes together." Sosa made a point.

"I agree with you, but my brother speaks very highly of you and that's why I'm here. I want to finish off where Roddy left off," Wayne stated, letting it be known he was down with the crew.

"Fair. We had been handling all the drug operations with Kaba. He's business minded and on point when it's time to collect and pick up," Sosa told him.

"I agree, but my goal is to get rid of them Outlaw niggas. I'm gunning for them," Wayne stated.

"Ain't we all? So, if you need anything, my crew is your crew, but I got some shit in the making I'ma need your help on," Sosa says.

"Great. Just call me. I'll be around, soldier," Wayne said, turning to walk off.

"Before you go, Wayne, I just want to let you know Lez is family and I protect my family with my life." Sosa hoped Wayne could read between his lines.

"I never heard of him," Wayne said, walking off.

Sosa hoped there would be no problems with Wayne and Lez because that shit would only make shit worse.

CHAPTER 9
NORTHEAST, PHILLY

Gee had just gotten off work from a ten-hour shift on the construction site he had been working at since he'd been home from prison. Adjusting to society was the hardest part of coming home. The other day he went to see his sister's gravesite and cleaned off the tombstone, placing new flowers on it. Till this day he still couldn't believe his sister got killed while he was locked up. He remembered the day he got the news of his sister being killed. He cried in his cell for days. What really hurt him was hearing that his own friend killed her in a shootout on the block.

Gee hadn't seen Lez, Twin, Sosa, and Lil Hak since he went up state, so he hadn't gotten the chance to speak to them, and he didn't plan to. Whenever Gee saw any of them, it was on sight.

Walking into Oxford Circle he saw a bunch of Outlaw niggas posted up in the hood.

"Gee, that's you?" a voice said from in the crowd.

"Who dat, though?" Gee stated looking into the crowd. Then, he saw the nigga Max who he was locked up with in the county before going to prison.

"It's me. Max," says Max approaching Gee who he remembered from way back.

"What's going on? I ain't see you in a while, bro. It's good to see you," Gee said.

"I heard you was home. You still fucking with them Sosa Gang niggas?" Max knew Gee was down with them niggas.

"Nah, bro, I ain't fucking with them clowns, dawg."

"Damn, it's like that?" Max smirked.

"Straight like that. Them niggas cross me, I'ma catch dem."

"If you need anything, I got you, bro. Facts. Just say the word, we out here, young bull," Max told him.

"Good looking, bro, but I'm working and trying to keep my head above water," Gee said, looking at Max's jewelry, thinking back to the days he used to get money with his Sosa Gang crew.

"Iight, bro, just say the word." Max turned and walked off.

Gee walked to his girlfriend's building thinking about Max offering a helping hand. He knew Max was crazy with the pistol and if he teamed up with him, then he may have a chance to go against Sosa Gang.

His girlfriend's crib smelled like cherry candles when he walked inside, taking off his shoes to see her in the living room praying.

Latifah was a devoted Muslim, and he loved that about her aside from her being a good woman. Finishing up her prayer, she gave Gee a hug. "Hey, babe." She kissed his lips.

"I missed you," he said, sitting on the couch getting comfortable.

"You did, huh?" she asked, climbing between his legs.

"Facts, babe," he said, looking at her hardened nipples.

"I can't tell." Latifah saw his penis about to bust out his work pants so she did him a favor and unzipped his fly and stroked his manhood on her knees.

"You playing games," he said, seeing his penis growing.

"I know what you want, daddy," she says, slowly licking his shaft up and down before engulfing his whole piece. She sucked his cock with passion until Gee nutted all over the leather couch.

Gee and Latifah fucked on the couch, both climaxing and falling asleep in the living room.

***

FISHTOWN, PA

Foxy was waiting on her dad to arrive so they could finally have a real one-on-one, face-to-face instead of on the phone and letters.

Growing up without having a father there was hard on her but she learned to manage thanks to her family members. Lez was the closest thing to a father figure beside her little brother Dawgy who Sosa Gang killed. Foxy was now grown and focused on business. She didn't care for a father and daughter relationship. She just wanted to chase money, not lost times.

It was chilly out today, so she had on a Valentino sweater with a hat to match. A Yukon SUV parked next to her Audi near the waterfront. She sat there patiently waiting on her dad, looking behind her shoulder to see Kane approaching.

"Hey, baby girl," Kane said, looking at how older and beautiful his daughter got over the years when he used to see her in pictures.

"Let's not do that. I'm here to get straight to the point. I'm a leading, active member of the Outlaws and I need you to supply me, and I'm well aware of the war and everything else taking place. I have my own money, and I'ma be loyal to the core. You have my number. Call me when your able to prepare the shipment and I will have my people meet your people. Take care," Foxy said with a stern face, getting up to leave.

Kane sat there listening, knowing she was a female version of him. Kane wasn't even mad about why she was acting this way because he popped back into her life after all these years, so it would take a while to get in good with her.

CHAPTER 10
UPTOWN, PHILLY

Karlee drove Sosa's Bentley to run a few errands around town to give Sosa a surprise birthday party with all of his friends she knew about. Sosa's sister was going help set it up when she got out of college in a few hours. It was still early so she had time to get everything together. She already rented out a ballroom to throw the party a few blocks away. She hired a DJ, caterer, and party designer to hook up the ballroom. She had been waiting for him to pop the question because she really wanted to spend the rest of her life with him and have a family with Sosa.

The cake store was to her right, so she figured his birthday cake was done for later. Karlee ordered a cake designed into a money machine with money logos attached to it. She saw a few people entering the store so hurried up and rushed inside.

"Damn it." Karlee saw her cousin calling her from jail, but she didn't have time to talk about his prison problems at the moment. "Excuse me. My name Karlee and I ordered a cake some hours ago," she said to one of the ladies behind the counter, skipping two dudes.

"The name of person the cake is for is what we go by, Miss?" A fat white lady replied.

"Sosa, my husband. Is that good enough?" Karlee sucked her teeth, catching an attitude. She had no patience today for people's bullshit.

"I'll go check on it." The fat lady rolled her eyes.

Karlee turned around to see the two dudes she skipped in line ice grilling her with nasty looks. "I'm sorry. I have my car running," Karlee lied, trying to ease the tension.

"You straight. We was just leaving," one of the dudes said before walking out.

"Fuck you, too," Karlee mumbled under her breath.

"Miss, here is your order," the fat lady who ran the store stated, bringing out a large box for Karlee.

"Thank you," Karlee says, taking the cake. She already sent a CashApp deposit to the store hours ago when she put in the order for it. Now Karlee had to go shopping and find herself a nice outfit for tonight. She wanted Sosa to have the best birthday of his young life.

Walking outside she didn't realize how heavy the cake really was until she made it to the middle of the parking lot.

"Yo, bitch!" a male voice shouted, making her look back, about to curse a nigga out, but what she saw next made her forget what Karlee had on her mind.

Bloc ... Bloc ... Bloc ... Bloc ... Bloc ... Bloc ... Bloc ... Bloc ...

The Hellcat OSP Desert FDE 9-millimeter handgun's 12-round micro compact bullets entered Karlee's back and neck. The cake flew in the air, fell on the ground, and some landed on Karlee as she died slowly.

Rizzy and his young bull ran off to their car, getting the fuck away from the nasty crime scene. Rizzy heard Karlee mention Sosa's name inside the cake store when he was in there to order a cake for his nephew's birthday. Hearing her say Sosa was her husband made him plot a quick successful plan to send Sosa a message. Seeing her lay dead next to a cake made him feel good but that wasn't enough. He wanted real blood from his ops.

***

DOWNTOWN, PHILLY

Sosa got a call from Karlee's sister telling him she was at Temple Hospital, claiming Karlee's dead body. Hearing Karlee being dead made him weak in his knees to the point he couldn't even move. Luckily Twin was with him when he got the call, so they were on their way to the hospital, speeding through traffic.

Twin saw his boy was in the passenger's seat, zoned out, rocking back and forth in the his seat. "It's gonna be aight, bro," Twin said, knowing that pain his friend was feeling now because Twin felt it before.

Sosa didn't say a word as all types of thoughts flooded his head, but he kept telling himself Karlee was alive.

When they got to the hospital, Sosa jumped out the moving car, running inside to see Karlee's sister and a few other people in the lobby signing papers. "What happened? Where is she?" Sosa shouted as everybody looked at him with glossy and puffy eyes from crying.

"She's dead, Sosa. I'm sorry," Karlee's sister said, seeing that he didn't understand.

"How?" Sosa asked.

"She got killed with your birthday cake in her hand, Sosa. Some gangstas killed her. If she would've focused on school and her career, she wouldn't be dead." Shr had tears rolling down her pretty face as she left with her family.

Sosa was crying as he took a seat when Twin arrived to comfort him. Twin knew Sosa loved that woman to death, so he already read Sosa's mind that somebody was about to pay for this.

Romell Tukes

CHAPTER 11
DOWNTOWN, PHILLY
TWO WEEKS LATER...

Barry's girlfriend worked at a new law firm and she upgraded from a paralegal to a real lawyer. Elia was the only black chick in the office, but she didn't mind; this was normal for her. She needed to get her clients up because right now she was taking courthouse cases.

"Excuse me. Ms. Elia, someone is out here asking for you," an older, pretty, petite white woman said, peeping her head inside Elia's office.

"Are you sure they're requesting me?" Elia asked with a confused look up on her face because she wasn't expecting anybody.

"Yes." The woman walked off with a strut. All the lawyers in the firm at least fucked her once or twice.

Elia saw Sosa walk in and she smiled, seeing her man's son stop by. "Sosa, what a big surprise?" She blushed.

"I heard you worked up here and I need to have a lawyer on retainer. A new one. So, I came to see if you're willing to take that role. I'ma warn you. A lot of my guys get locked up daily and I'ma need you to go get them out. I'ma always be able to send you whatever amount needed on CashApp or whatever will be easy for you. I just don't like my people to be sitting in lock-up thinking I'm not finna get dem out. That's when people feel abandoned and start doing things," Sosa said, seeing Elia nod her head, already knowing what he was getting at.

"I understand. We can get it started, but I need to know how much are you putting down?" Elia asked, pulling out some papers.

"Two hundred and fifty thousand," Sosa said, handing her a debit card with that amount of money on it.

"Okay. Credit card. It's perfect. I just need you to fill out some papers then everything is in motion," she said, seeing a few attorneys peek in her office with jealous looks because she'd just started and already had clients coming.

***

WESTSIDE, PHILLY

Foxy had a few women in an apartment, breaking keys down, cooking coke, turning it into crack, and bagging up dime, dubs, and ounces to sell throughout the Westside. The Outlaws had a few blocks on this side of town she was going to flood with work. Rika was gonna reach out to a few people she knew out of town as well.

"Girl, we about to have the city looking like the eighties out here," Rika stated, watching the chicks cut the drugs like pros.

"It's light, but you and Beth are my two capo's. I need y'all to focus and help me get to this bag. I want us to be the female version of BMF," Foxy stated, looking at the forty plus keys on the table scattered all over the place.

"Girl, that sounds good but a bitch ain't trying to get that Big Meech time," Rika joked. But she was serious.

"Don't be flashy," Foxy said, knowing that was Southwest T and Big Meech's downfall.

"You right. But I ain't know you had it made like this," Rika says.

"That's how it supposed to be." Foxy laughed.

"Beth is on the southside about to do her thing. She said niggas is too deep out there, but she about to bait him in," Rika says, reading her sister's text she had just got.

"Iight. She'll do good. It's an easy job," Foxy said, feeling her stomach hurt due to her period, so she left and headed home to her new condo to get some rest.

***

SOUTH PHILLY

The block was popping today. Everybody came out to a neighborhood called CAPA where shit was always live and turned up. Lil Jet and ten other Sosa Gang members trapped in front of the store on the block all day. Lil Jet was raised around these parts, so everybody knew him and respected his gun game, even the old G's. Thanks to Twin, the whole block was getting money. Big money—

moving ounces, grams, and quarters, half-keys and whole chickens. Whichever a nigga needed, they had it on this side.

A BMW sedan pulled up in front of them, and a bad, slim, brown chick hopped out, making all of them look, even Lil Jet who was sitting near the door of the store. Everybody tried to get her attention, but she respectfully nodded until she saw Lil Jet. She smiled and walked into the store to cop a pack of cigarettes. Lil Jet felt the chick's vibe, so he went in the store behind her, liking the way her jeans fit her nice ass.

"Hey," she says.

"You not from this side," Lil Jet said seeing how sexy she was up close.

"Nah. Why? Does it matter?"

"Not at all. I'm Lil Jet."

"I'm Ri."

"How about you make some time for a playa so we can vibe together and build," Lil Jet asked, trying to bag her when seeing her smile.

"Okay. Here." She gave him her number and put her real number in his phone with her stage name Ri because her real name was Rika.

***

WEST, PHILLY
A DAY LATER

Lez and Brad sat in the car talking while watching a block that belonged to the Outlaws, trying to map out the way they moved.

"Is it me or does it look like them chicks over there selling more weight than the niggas?" Brad stated.

"You must've read my mind, bull," Lez said, watching the same thing, wondering who would let chicks move drugs on the block.

"This shit looking weird out here." Brad shook his head, about to roll up a blunt.

"Facts. I think something is going on that we don't know about, but I'ma find out."

CHAPTER 12
DOWNTOWN PHILLY

The DEA building was next to the main courthouse and Janasia was one of the main DEA agents there. She was also the youngest and hardest worker at the office. At twenty-nine years old she was well established with her career. Her childhood was not the best, but she made it work with the little she did have.

Janasia's father was gunned down in the streets by a crazy man who had a bad day and spazzed out. Her mom was a nurse to feed her boys and little girl. Growing up with two brothers under one roof being the only girl made her tough. When she went to college in North Carolina her life elevated at Duke University where she started studying two majors. There wasn't a day that went by where she didn't feel grateful for where she came from which was South Philly.

Janasia was a beautiful woman with flawless coco brown skin, curves, long hair, and white teeth for her nice smile. With a busy life due to work she had no time for relationships. As long as her big black dildo had batteries, she felt good.

It was 6:30PM, and normally she would've been home if she wasn't working overnight. Tonight, her caseload was thick. A few murders had been going on lately and she wanted to get to the bottom of it. A few of her rats told her there was a big war going with Sosa Gang and the Outlaws since an OG nigga came home. Janasia did her research on this OG cat and the streets called him Kane. Looking through his files tonight, she could tell that he a serious killer. Even in jail he beat two murders for stabbing two inmates to death.

She wanted to look more into the Sosa Gang kids because she had been hearing their name a lot lately in the streets. One of her co-workers told her the Sosa Gang was the reason for 17% percent of the city's murders. Her boss gave her this case because he or anyone else couldn't crack it. It was just too much, and the feds claimed the gang wasn't on their radar anymore.

In a few days she would be turning 30 years old. She couldn't wait because she made plans to go on a trip with a few of her girlfriends.

***

DOWNTOWN, PHILLY

Sosa drove to the airport to pick up his dad from Southwest Airlines. His dad's flight landed two minutes ago so he was speeding through traffic.

The other day he had to watch Karlee get buried and that crushed his heart to the highest level because Karlee was the love of his life. He thought all women were out for money and clout but Karlee showed him different. She made him realize that there were good black strong women out there looking for their kings.

He needed to speak to his pops about last week's shipment. He got the product stepped on and people were complaining. It wasn't the regular product he had been getting so this needed to be addressed.

Parking in front of the main entrance he saw a Maserati coupe with the top down in front of him. Sosa liked Maseratis. They were nice cars, fast and classy. The woman he saw inside the driver's seat looked Spanish and beautiful.

Sosa got out the Hellcat and walked inside the airport. On his way past a search-point he saw a sexy dark-skinned woman. For some reason, her features reminded him of Karlee, but the woman he was staring at had bright green eyes as if she wore colorful contacts. Something about her gave him goosebumps. They made eye contact and Sosa quickly turned his head nervously, not trying to have a stare down in the middle of a packed airport. Sosa still didn't see Barry, but he did see the beautiful woman coming his way and his heart started to race to a new beat.

"Pardon me, sir. I need some help, and I see you just standing there staring, so why not help?" The beautiful smiled and quickly won his heart as if Karlee never had it.

Sosa was so stuck he just nodded and helped her with all her bags and luggage she was carrying which was enough for two people.

"Thank you. What's your name?" She asked as they looked like a cute couple walking through the main lobby.

"Sosa."

"I'm Allure. That's also my IG and Facebook name," she stated to make sure he caught her drift.

"Okay. I'll make sure I will DM you," he told her.

"Cool, but this is my ride," Allure says, walking out the sliding doors toward the nice Maserati coupe. The woman hopped out the driver seat with a fat ass and a flat tummy. He thought it was Allure's sister.

"Should I put these in your backseat?" Sosa asked, seeing the driver pop the trunk.

"Yes, please. Hey, mom," Allure said as she hugged the woman.

Sosa couldn't believe the sexy lady was her mom because her mom looked Spanish and Allure skin was dark as if she was African. "There you go," Sosa said, placing the last bag in the backseat.

"Thank you so much. Hit me in the DM as soon as you can. I owe you one," Allure said with a wink before getting in the passenger seat of the car.

"I will, trust me," Sosa repeated before the car pulled off. This was the first time he smiled since losing Karlee and he knew she would want him to be happy. Sosa checked his watch, seeing his dad was twenty-five minutes late. Looking through the glass door he finally saw Barry coming his way in a Versace outfit, gold and white; it was clean. "You got lost?" Sosa asked, seeing his dad with one small bag. Barry always traveled light.

"Sorry, son. My flight was late," Barry says, getting inside Sosa's Hellcat. He liked the little fast car.

"It's good, but I'm glad you called me because that last shit you gave me sucked. It was stepped on."

"Are you serious?" Barry asked, getting upset.

"Yeah. I wouldn't lie about that."

"Okay. I'ma make it up to you. Sorry. My plug was overseas, so I went to someone else. I should've told you."

"It's all good."

"I'ma handle it. Trust me," Barry stated with a stern tone, thinking about the blood he was finna shed over the disrespect.

CHAPTER 13
TEMPLE UNIVERSITY COLLEGE, PHILLY

Zarhya had a busy day today. It's a new semester and she had to purchase new textbooks and school supplies. She waited in the long line outside of the school's canteen building. With her second year at the college, Zarhya loved everything the school had to offer. Keeping all A's and B's wasn't easy at all, but she studied four or more hours every day. Sometimes she pulled all-nighters studying for exams and tests. Her brother Sosa and dad made sure she was good financially which was a blessing because working a part time job and completing school was a hard task. She saw women do this daily and eventually they ended up dropping out of school to focus on money.

"Zarhya, this line long as shit," Curt said behind her.

"I know, right." Zarhya used to see blocks like this filled with feins waiting on there early morning hits on her way to school in southwest Philly.

"You going out with that dude I saw you with the other day in that black Benz?" Curt asked, being noisy because he liked her, but she didn't give none of the college boys a shot. Zarhya saw how they ran chicks' names in the ground after having sexual relations with them.

"Don't, Curt. Mind yours."

"May bad."

"Plus, you got a girl. And ain't she pregnant right now?" Zarhya asked.

"Yeah, she is." Curt felt bad.

"Boy, niggas is grimy." She laughed.

"You heard what happened to that chick that went to school here?"

"Karlee." Zarhya stated sadly, already knowing what happened. Karlee was an active student. Everybody loved her.

"Yeah. I remember she used to be with you a lot," Curt said.

When Zarhya heard about Karlee's death, it was all over the school and she cried all night long. A few weeks before Karlee got killed, they went out to eat and to catch a movie, having a girls night out.

As the line started to move, so did her thought about Karlee. Curt kept talking but all she saw were lips moving as she thought about the good times she and Karlee shared.

***

WEST PHILLY

Brad had his seat leaned all the way back in the Toyota, listening to a Lox album, his favorite rap group. For a young nigga, Brad had good taste in music. He loved old school mid-90's music.

He watched four young ladies on the block laugh and have a good time drinking Lean and smoking weed, just chilling. Brad knew that was their cover because he saw them do hand to hand drug sells for hours.

The girls were selling drugs to feins, bustlers, and rich clients coming through in luxury cars all day. He just got off the phone with Lez, telling him this, and Lez knew somebody smart was running the show from the Outlaws.

Lez wanted Kane for killing his brother Kilow who was a dirty cop. Brad knew in six hours the chicks on the block across the street had to make over $50,000 at the least.

It was dark out, so he knew it was time to go. Lez told him it would be smart to hang around past 9 for safety purposes because they wanted to keep a low profile.

When he leaned forward to turn on the car, a female popped up at the driver's side, scaring the shit out of him. Before he had a chance to roll down the window for the pretty woman who seemed lost, she lifted her Glock 32.

Boc...Boc...Boc...Boc...Boc...Boc...Boc...Boc...

Beth ran off down the block after shooting him in his face, going into overkill. The girls on the block worked for Beth and told her someone in a Toyota was watching them close at the end of the block across the street. Beth played the cut and watched the Toyota for over an hour and she figured it was a jackboy trying to hit a lick. Beth was not going for it, so she pulled her move.

By the time police arrived, Brad was slumped in the driver's seat dead, soaked in blood with holes in his face.

***

NORTHEAST PHILLY

Gee just quit his job. He was sick of doing construction and kissing the white man's ass, so he walked off the site. He walked into Oxford Circle to see Max leaning on a new Infiniti Q60 two-door super coupe on rims. Since his last convo with Max, he had been thinking it was time he put his plan in motion. "Ayo, Max, you got a second," Gee said into the small crowd of young wolves surrounding Max as if he was their God.

"What up, bull?"

"Take a walk with me," Gee stated, seeing Max get off the car.

"My boy Gee. What up, bruh? Good to see you."

"I had been thinking about our last conversation and I wanna get down." Gee got straight to the point.

"What made you come to that decision?" Max wanted to know because Gee used to be one of the main Sosa Gang niggas.

"Dem niggas killed my sister, so it's beef forever, and I need to get this money, bro," Gee stated seriously.

"Aight. I respect that. Welcome to the Outlaws." Max embraced Gee, welcoming him to the family.

"Facts. I'ma put on," Gee added.

"I got a block I want you to run in southwest. You know we got a few hoods over there we get money in, bull. But I'ma have you hold down Larchwood Projects because the young bulls Painy and Ridera got snatched up for two bodies last night they did last year," Max said.

"Sosa Gang niggas be over there, too?" Gee asked, knowing Lil Hak used to run that area.

"They be up the block, but the bull Lil Hak had been gone for a while now, so we took over the projects."

"I got 'cha."

"I know. I'ma give you three keys. One is for your own sake, and the rest we bust down seventy-thirty," Max said.

"Damn. Why not sixty-forty, bro? I'ma be making pennies," Gee says, not feeling the profit.

"Seventy-thirty is good when you getting dem joints left and right."

"Facts," Gee stated, adding it up. If he was to move five to ten keys a week, he would be up in no time.

***

SPRINGFIELD, PA

On the outskirts of Philly, detective Ball had a three-story house where she lived on the bottom section. She got off work at 10 tonight after a long day. She did two drug raids and a murder arrest. All her years on the force, she'd never seen so many murders in Philly as she did between this year and the last. July 4th was in a few days, and she knew the city would rack up at least 227 murders altogether from the beginning of January. She made it to her home drained, ready to hit the sack, but first she planned to take a shower.

The moment she stepped foot in her crib, two men snatched her up, overpowering her. They slammed the front door and dragged her into the living room to their boss.

"What the fuck is going on?" she yelled before the living room lamp came on and she saw Barry sitting down in a Dior for men suit.

"Ball, you played me. After all these years you cross me up, huh?" Barry's voice was calm.

"Barry, what are you talking about?" She had no clue as to what he was getting at and why he was in her home.

"Dem three hundred keys of cut you sold me. Bitch, don't play with me!" Barry shouted.

Detective Ball had a side job which was stealing drugs from the evidence room and robbing local drug dealers. When she racked up 300 keys of coke, the first person to enter her mind was Barry. She was Barry's eyes and ears. Since she became a cop, she had been his dirty cop and insider. "Barry, I got those drugs from work. I swear I ain't know it was cut," Ball defended herself.

"Too late."

"After all I did for you, you think I would cross you, Barry? Come on!" She cried out.

"People change with time."

"Okay. I'll make it up," she said.

"No second chances. The next time would fall back on me, now, wouldn't it?"

"I know who robbed your hala store a while back." Ball caught his attention because she knew he was inquiring about it.

"Ball, don't fucking play with me."

"I'm not, Barry. I had my people find footage of the night it happened. The camera across the street from the hala shop at the post office caught your ex-wife and four men leaving out with duffle bags," Ball said.

Barry saw the sincere look in her face and for some reason he believed her.

Boc…Boc…

Barry shot her in the neck, walking out her house, thinking about his ex-wife he hadn't seen in years.

Romell Tukes

CHAPTER 14
NEW JERSEY

OG Kane took his wife out to a nice, classy hotel outside of Atlantic City in New Jersey to spend some time with her, and they couldn't get enough of sex. Vera and Kane had just come back to the penthouse from having a good dinner.

Vera was a pretty Hispanic woman, thick in all the right places, and she did real estate for over ten years now. She knew Kane for a long time, and they got married while he was in prison. To have him home was big. She couldn't stop smiling. No man never made her feel as good as Kane did. He always found a way to make her feel like a queen. "That was delicious, baby," Vera said, laying her Chanel purse on the kitchen table.

"I was staring at you in that sexy dress the whole time. I couldn't even focus on the food," Kane stated looking at her teal Alexandre Vauttier one-piece and high heels.

"You were." She followed him to the master bedroom that had a hot tube in the middle of the floor.

Kane already had a hard-on from looking at her curvy body all day. "Yeah. Now, strip for me." He leaned back on the bed as she slowly undressed, exposing her nice size breasts then her fat, shaved cunt.

She climbed between his legs and started to undress him while humming until they were both perfectly naked. Vera straddled his lap, slowly sinking onto his manhood as he opened her tightness. "Oh my God." She moaned as he caught her pace, sliding up and down on the pipe as he sucked her nipples like candy. Vera was so wet that she already had the sheets soaked with her juices. His cock went deep into her tight little hole while gripping her waist. The impact was so strong she couldn't control her climax as she came hard.

"That's right," Kane said, seeing her cum on his cock as she continued to bounce up and down.

Vera then got on her hands and knees on the bed, arching her back.

Kane wasted no time in getting behind her to fill her up with his loving.

"Fuck me!" She screamed loudly as his cock impaled her.

Kane loved the way her pussy tightened when she was taking dick.

"Ugghhhh." Vera grunted and moaned, lost in a haze of arousal as he continued to pound her pussy while she screamed out in pleasure. Vera let him nut in her tiny hole but when he came, she wanted to taste some. So, she opened her mouth and licked the tip of his pole. She moved her lips along his length, then bobbed her head.

He thrusted his penis down her throat, hitting the back of her throat until he came long and hard.

"Let's fuck in the hot tub," she requested, and he couldn't resist.

"Okay," he said, looking at her ass bounce, ready for round two, gassing himself up.

***

West Philly

Lez, Twin, and Lil Jet were chopping it up about the recent events going on in the gang.

"Are you sure some bitches killed him, bro?" Twin asked after hearing some chicks opening shop on Lez's side of town.

"Bull, we was watching dem hoes close, and all of a sudden he got killed on their block, bro. I know they had something to do with it," Lez said.

"Niggas be sleeping on bitches nowadays. Shit, they more vicious than us, bro," Lil Jet said, seeing Lez's block do numbers with feins flooding the area.

"You think they got a connection to dem chicks who tried to kill me?" Twin asked, thinking about what happened to him a while back when a chick tried to line him up.

"I don't know. I'ma find out," Lez says.

"I believe Lil Hak back. Sosa texted me last night," Twin said.

"Good, we need the bull back," Lez said, happy to hear his boy was back in town.

"He should be good on that cop killing though," Twin told Lez.

"Lil Hak was good from the yata, bro. Facts." Lil Jet knew about the event because he saw the cop killing all over the news.

"I gotta meet up with Wayne in a few," Twin said, checking his watch, forgetting Lez disliked Wayne.

"Y'all really fucking with dude?" Lez asked.

"I'm saying its business, and dem niggas coming through for us. Bro, them niggas good people. You have to learn how to forgive people," Twin stated, walking off.

"You talking outta all people? I saw you pistol-whip a nigga two months ago outside of that bar because he used to bully you in school," Lez reminded him.

"I'm emotionally scarred over that." Twin laughed.

"Fuck outta here," Lez said, climbing on his bike, thinking about who killed Brad.

***

SOUTHWEST PHILLY
ONE MONTH LATER

"Ayo, Sosa. This shit is starting to fuck my head up," Lil Hak said as both men walked into the fast-food restaurant to grab a bite to eat. Lil Hak heard some Outlaw niggas recently took over his block and he was pissed about that.

"I'm saying, bro, you was gone for a while. That was the only hood we couldn't lock down because we ain't have enough niggas over there," Sosa admitted, about to order some salad because he had been back on his healthy shit.

"Larchwood always had been our stomping grounds."

"It wasn't no money when you left, bro. Everything left when you went away," Sosa told him.

"Now it's jumping again."

"So, get your block back, nigga. It's simple. Take some niggas and put it on, southwest style," Sosa told him because he was already sick of Lil Hak talking about a dead block that used to be live and fill of money.

"Iight. I'ma do that," Lil Hak said. "It's good to be back, though, bull. I was getting sick of being outta town." He saw three dudes enter the McDonald's, staring at him and Sosa.

Sosa looked at Rizzy and shit went left inside McDonald's. Rizzy went for his Glock the same time Sosa did. All the employees saw the commotion and already knew what was going on.

Bloc... Bloc... Bloc... Bloc... Bloc... Bloc...

Sosa hit one of Rizzy's goons in the dome while Rizzy grazed Lil Hak in his left arm before ducking off behind the counter.

Boc... Boc...

Sosa was gunning for Rizzy who weaved the bullets, crawling to the nearest exit once he saw his last man go down. He knew there wouldn't be any possible chance of him making it out alive with both of them on his ass like this. Rizzy crawled out the back, slipping on hamburger grease while bullets still flew everywhere. When he made it out back, he dashed to his car and Sosa and Lil Hak met him out there, not giving up.

Boc...Boc...Boc...Boc...Boc...Boc...Boc...Boc ...

Luckily, Rizzy made it out untouched; only with a few holes in his car.

CHAPTER 15
NORTH PHILLY

Lez recently buried Lil Brad the other day and he was pissed off about his little cousin's death. He didn't know for sure if them chicks killed Brad. Today he was focused on Max because word on the street is Max had relations with the man who killed his brother. Finding out OG Kane killed Kilow didn't sit well with him. Even though Lez and Kilow had no type of relationship, he was still blood. If he could get at Max and find a way to make him five up OG Kane, then his real mission would soon begin.

Max was a few cars ahead in a new nice-looking Porsche with an older woman who looked pretty for her age.

Lez listened to a PNB Rock classic album thinking of how he should let his bad vibes with Wayne go because that was a long time ago. Plus, now that his crew allies with the D.C. Crew he knew it would be fair to let bygones be bygones.

He watched the car pull into a high school parking lot which was completely empty on this Sunday morning. All of a sudden, something crazy happened that he didn't expect, as he tried to keep a distance from the car that had also entered the parking lot. Max jumped out the driver's side with a gun and his hand.

Lez parked and quickly slid out his Dodge charger with a Mack 10 submachine gun in hand.

Tat… Tat… Tat… Tat… Tat… Tat… Tat…

Bloc… Bloc… Bloc… Bloc…

The two men exchanged gunfire in the empty high school parking lot.

Max took cover behind the driver door, shooting back at Lez but missing his target each shot.

While driving, he peeped the blue Charger tailing him for a few minutes, so in his mind, he knew it was an op. If the car tailing him was a cop then most likely Max knew he would've gotten pulled over when he ran two stop signs and a red light on purpose.

Tat… Tat… Tat… Tat… Tat…

Bloc… Bloc…

Max thought he caught Lez with his last bullet until he came out of nowhere, letting it rip again. He climbed in the Porsche driver seat filled with pieces of glass and pulled off, but he didn't realize his aunty caught two head taps. "Shittt!" he yelled, racing away from the murder scene with no windows.

Being that his aunt was an off-duty police officer in Philly's 65th district, her death was about to bring mad heat from every police department in the city. Lez and Max weren't ready for what was about to come with this murder.

***

DOWNTOWN PHILLY

DEA agent Ms. Janasia came out to a low-key cafe to have some coffee this morning before going off to work. She came here not only to enjoy her morning coffee but to also speak to one of her informants. The murder of a former off-duty cop was all over the news and newspapers. It got her upset to the point where she wanted to pull up on blocks to find out who did it.

There was so much going on in the city with police killing young blacks and now people killing black police officers who were trying to help and defuse the violence in the city. She still had been working night and day on her caseload, but the main problem Janasia had been coming across is matching the faces, names, and locations of the men she did have on her radar.

Her guest finally walked in carrying a sleeping baby in her arms.

"Hi, you must be Takeela," Janasia asked, pulling out a chair for the woman.

"Yes, I am." Takeela sat down, cuddling her baby.

"You called me saying that you had some info on the police killing that recently took place." Janasia looked into the young ladies dark eyes, seeing she had two small black eyes as if someone punched her in the face.

"Yeah, I did."

"Okay, so let's start from point A. Who did it?"

"Dem Sosa Gang dudes," Takeela says with no shame for going against the street code.

"How do you know this, Takeela?"

"My deadbeat baby father is at war with dem."

"So, your baby father is an Outlaw member?" Janasia asked.

"Yes."

"What's his name?"

"Max."

When Janasia heard the name, she knew off the rip who the kid was from her files. He was a big-time troublemaker. He was also wanted for a few murders but had only been questioned because the Philly 55th Precinct and the 8th Precinct homicide officers could never tie Max to any of the cases for some reason. "How do you know Max is at war?" Janasia wanted to know everything so she could put the pieces of the puzzle together.

"Max and I used to talk all the time. He used to tell me everything after I fucked him and sucked his dick, to be honest. He told me a big war was going down since his big homie OG Kane came home."

"OG Kane?" Janasia asked.

"Yeah. He ran the Outlaws, I think."

"Do you know why they're beefing?"

"Not really. Max don't even really know, but I know he always talk about taking over Philly."

"Do you know any Sosa Gang leaders?" Janasia needed to really know this.

"Yeah."

"Who are they?"

"Lez, Twin, and I think the main dude name is Sosa," Takeela stated.

"Sosa?"

"Yeah."

But that's their crew name, Janasia thought. It didn't make sense.

"That's what Max says. The main kid's name is Sosa, and he doing big things."

"What type of big things?" Janasia wanted clarity.

"I heard he moving bricks all over. Sosa Gang is the biggest gang in the city, so for him to feed all those hoodlums, he must be on a big level," Takeela says, seeing her baby's eyes open slowly.

"That's his baby?"

"Yeah, but he not claiming it. He says I'm a thot and was with other dudes while I was fucking him, but everybody says he look like Max."

"I'm sure he'll come around," Janasia replied, feeling sad for the young lady.

"If dem niggas don't kill him… because Sosa Gang serious. They killed two of my cousins in the same day, and you see how they did Max aunty." Takeela shook her head.

"Who is Max's aunty?"

"The cop lady who just got killed," Takeela said, checking her G-shock watch because she had to go take a GED test. Takeela dropped out the 12th grade two years ago because of family problems.

Janasia couldn't believe Max's aunt was the officer that got killed by his ops. "Thank you, Takeela. If anything comes up, please give me a call."

"I don't think that would be smart. I just fear for Max's life. Even though he did me fucked up, I still think he's my child father," Takeela says, getting up to leave.

Janasia couldn't believe what she was hearing. Now, it was all starting to come together.

***

SOUTH PHILLY

Lil Jet finished taking a shower at his new apartment with his girl Parie— a slim, dark-skinned chick with piercings all over her body, but it looked cute on her. The two knew each other for a while but just recently started a relationship, and the sex was popping.

"Damn, you get some good dick and knock out," Lil Jet says walking back into the room to get dressed.

"Nigga, you know what you be doing," Parie stated.

"I hear you."

"Where you going?"

"I have to meet up with my boy real quick. You can chill here."

"I bet ya would love for me to lay here so you can come back and fuck the shit outta me again," Parie said, getting out the bed to get ready for work at a bar to service bottles. She was only 19 years old but acted grown.

"I'll come to your job and bang your little box out," he said.

"We not doing that again." She laughed, remembering the time he came to her job and had sex with her in the back area.

"Call me when you get off," he told her.

"You know I will, daddy." She began to get dressed, thinking of how blessed her life was now besides her aunty recently being killed.

CHAPTER 16
CENTER CITY, PHILLY

Lil Brad's death pointed fingers in a lot of people's directions, but there was one person Lez couldn't exclude and that's why he was waiting in this hair salon parking lot in front of a pink Audi he knew belonged to Foxy because she loved the color pink. He knew every Friday she came here to get her nails and hair done for years. There were Fridays he would have to take her down when she didn't have a car.

Seeing the expensive luxury car, he started to wonder what she was into nowadays to be able to afford this type of car. It wasn't his place to question her because they weren't together, but he was dying to know.

Foxy walked out on her iPhone on Facetime with someone, laughing, joking, having a great time. When she lifted her head to see Lez in front of her, she paused, then quickly hung up. "You clocking me or something?" Foxy stated as her blood boiled just by looking at him.

"We need to talk."

"No, we don't need to talk, but I do need to get in my fucking car," she stated, unable to look him in the eyes.

"My little cousin Lil Brad got killed around our way by some chick, and I'm trying to see if you can help."

"Sorry, Lez. I don't know nothing about what you're saying. You should call 1-900-crime-stoppers," she shot back rudely as she thought back to the time she asked him for help on her brother's murder.

"It's like that?"

"You lucky I'm fucking nice about it because I wanna tell you to get the fuck outta my face," she says seriously.

"Aight."

"You don't have your people scoping out mutherfucker's blocks?" Foxy exposed her hand.

"Okay," Lez says, letting everything she just said soak in.

"You play with the devil, better believe eventually karma gonna come right back." Foxy got in her car talking shit as Lez stood there.

"I guess the devil wear Prada heels, too." Lez knew Foxy had a big part in his little cousin's murder.

"Yep. Now, can you excuse me?" she asked nicely.

"I'ma tell you this, my nigga. When you on the devil's playground, leave your angels in heaven, because I'm rolling wit some demons."

"I can get on demon time, too, Lez. You ain't see shit yet." Foxy pulled off, unaware she told Lez everything he needed to know.

"That bitch," Lez mumbled, piecing everything up from their whole little conversation.

Foxy was doing big things and he planned to dig a little more into her personal life first so he could see what was missing or different.

Lez got in his car and called Sosa to get some more input on this Foxy situation, but one thing he couldn't miss was how good she was looking. The whole time he spent talking to her he, had an erection and he knew she had to see it.

***

UPTOWN PHILLY

Lil Jet had sweat dripping down his forehead as he just nutted on his side chick's round ass. She had some of the best pussy he ever had in his life.

"Damn, daddy, you put it on a bitch tonight," his side bitch said, fucking up the backseats in her new Range Rover.

"You're the best."

"No, you're the best. Trust me, I don't even be fucking with young niggas, but shit, you be putting it on dis pussy," she stated getting dress.

"I'm only one year younger than you," he told her, laughing, looking at her perfect body.

"Whatever. You lucky I like you." She blushed as her legs continued to shake from the good fuck session.

"When you free again?"

"Hit my line whenever you want. I'm always free for you."

"Cool, but I see you copped a new truck. You stepping your game up I see." Lil Jet got in a train station parking.

"I'm trying to get like you." She thought Lil Jet was a scammer as he told everybody else.

"I'm at the bottom."

"Well, maybe one day we can climb to the top together."

"You never know," Lil Jet replied, kissing her lips before walking to his car.

The woman blushed, shaking her head, knowing she was catching feelings for the nigga she had been fucking for over two weeks. His dick was so good, every time she would tell herself, "No." Beth would always come back. This was the sixth sexual experience in days. She didn't know him by his nickname, only by Justin, his real name. She felt security and comfortable around him since the first day she met him in front of the store. She knew a job needed to be done, but Beth never caught feelings for someone so fast, even though he told her there was another woman. Beth knew no bitch could compare to her if she got serious about the man.

There was so much weight on Beth's mind, and she knew soon it would all be over. Beth had to keep her word to Foxy.

***

SOUTHWEST PHILLY

Lil Hak rocked a champion hoodie walking up the block where Larchwood Projects were. He saw feins running in and out in a rush, smiling and joyful. Going into his old projects would've been dumb, so Lil Hak played the background and stayed low key. "Ayo!" he shouted at a fein.

"Who dat?" The chick asked, looking to see who was under the hoodie and stopping her from going to cop her next hit of a one and one which is a bag of dope and crack.

"Me. Cuzzy Cherly, be quiet," Lil Hak told his older cousin who was a straight smoker.

"Oh, shit. Lil Hak, where you been at, cuz? Oh my God. Come give me a hug. Fuck, that let me get some money." She stuck her hand out with no type of shame.

"Who running dis shit?" Lil Hak asked, paying her begging no mind.

"What you mean?"

"Who controlling this shit?"

"Dem Outlaw niggas, I think. I remember when you and your crew used to run this shit. When you coming back?"

"Soon. But who is the main nigga?" Lil Hak hated asking his slow ass cousin shit because she only understood money, drugs, and getting high or selling ass for drugs.

"That kid who used to be wit you."

"Wit me?"

"Yeah."

"What's his name?" This was new to Lil Hak. He didn't have a clue who she spoke of.

"Gee."

"What? Gee from North?" Lil Hak was puzzled.

"Yeah. I think he from North Philly. I knew he was getting money with them Outlaw niggas," she stated.

"Aight. I have to go," Lil Hak says, rushing off as she still continued to ask for money.

***

DOWNTOWN PHILLY

Sosa needed some time to get his thoughts together because losing Karlee was still fresh on his mind and emotion. Since Karlee's death, he hadn't had a good night's sleep but he kept a game face on in front of people so nobody would see him sweat the pain and tears out. He had been at Karlee's gravesite for over thirty minutes and it was time to go. He got a small peace of mind whenever he came up here since Karlee's death.

On the way out, he saw someone standing nearby at another gravesite, staring at the grave which looked old with rust stains on the metal name plates.

78

"Your either bad at your job, or so thirsty you're moving sloppy," Sosa told the beautiful woman who had one of the prettiest faces he ever saw in his life.

"Excuse me, sir?" The woman sounded defensive.

"Those graves are from 1801, and they are a white couple. I can tell by their Russian names. I'm sure you don't know them. You had been following me for three days with nine small breaks in between, Miss. I don't know if you're a fed, homicide department, ATF, undercover, or a creep. I do know your name is Janasia. You live on Martin and Grant in a nice apartment, your social security number is 424-19-1801," Sosa said, seeing her crazy facial expression.

Janasia had no clue Sosa would be so on point, but now her life was in danger because he knew so much shit about her. When Sosa turned to walk off, she stopped him. "Okay. I'm a DEA agent investigating you and your gang. Y'all are the reason the city's murder rate is out the roof. You may know a little bit about me, but that won't stop me from sending your black ass off to prison," she assured him.

"I know," Sosa mumbled nonchalantly.

"The coroners are running outta room to put all these bodies, and you muthafuckas think it's a game."

"I want to bring peace, not murder, Ms. Janasia. I don't kill people. I let people kill themselves, but I won't hesitate to protect my loved ones. I'm not too confrontational, but apparently you are, and I can see why. You're beautiful, at work all day, and you want justice for what's right." Sosa's tone was slow and soft.

"You're damn right," she added.

"I'ma tell you this right now. Don't cross that line. This cemetery is filled with young, beautiful women like yourself." Sosa made an ideal threat and she caught it.

"Let me guess. You put them here, too?" She contested.

"Who knows. Women and kids are something we are against, but mistakes do happen. I'm sure you can testify to that." Sosa saw how perfect her facial features were.

"No, I can't. Sorry. And before I go, I want to let you know how dumb you are for teaming up with the D.C. Crew."

"Why is that?"

"I'm sure you will see before I do, boss man. I can't wait to nail you," she said, turning to walk off.

Sosa stood there for a few seconds thinking about what just happened. He had the DEA on his ass, but his dad warned him a while back. Now he needed to figure all of this shit out quick or she could bring down everything in one sweep.

***

A few niggas from the D.C. Crew were having a cookout at the park on 58th and Myers Street, enjoying the nice sunny day. Wayne and Kaba pulled off to the side so they could talk about everything that's had been going on with the crew and their allies.

"What's been up, bull? I ain't see you in a few weeks." Kaba said.

"I've been laying low, focusing on this money and getting Roddy settled in his new crib. He got one of his ex-girls back, so she is a lot of help to him which saves me a lot of time," Wayne says, happy his brother was out the hospital, but his in a wheelchair for life now.

"That what's good. I love that nigga. I gotta pull up on him later."

"Facts, but I'm supposed to go pick up that load tonight. I may need you to do it because I gotta go check some shit out in York, PA." Says Wayne.

"What's going on out there?"

"Chill, young bull." Wayne laughed

"You already making big moves fresh home, but what you think about the Sosa Gang niggas on our side?"

"I mean, it is what it is, bull. We getting money, so that's all I care about," Wayne admitted.

"You know in a few weeks there's going to be a big meeting wit everybody?"

"I heard already."

"Iight, cool, but I hope Sosa get some better work. The last shit had too much on it, bro."

"So I heard, but Sosa be having a lot going on. I think they had something to do with that cop killing shit."

"Oh, yeah. Dem police had been too quiet. They about to start shaking shit down." Kaba already knew how the Philly PD got when one of their own were gunned down.

"Fuck it. They want a war, we'll give them one," Wayne added.

"No lie."

"Let's enjoy this cookout. I'm starving right now, bro."

"Facts." Kaba was glad to have his boy back home. The crew never looked so good. Everybody was eating and that's thanks to Sosa.

***

DOWNTOWN PHILLY

Club Ace had all the hottest rappers and ballplayers come out to enjoy themselves and meet the cities baddest bitches. Foxy, Beth, and Rika all came out for a girl's night out on her, of course. The blocks she was taking over had been doing good, but she knew the fire dog food that was given to her had feins going wild.

She was supposed to meet up with her dad in a few days for her next load and she couldn't wait. Her encounter with Lez fucked up her train of thought. Foxy yearned to tell him she killed his little cousin since his people killed her brother, but she thought against it.

"Cheers to our new life." Foxy put her glass of champagne in the air as the club's lights hit her Rolex watch. They made a toast.

"Girl, we should've had been got into this field. I had been counting so much money my hands smell like blue faces," Rika stated, making the girls laugh.

"How is shit going with that Lil Jet kid?" Foxy asked Beth who was quiet all night in her sexy satin slim Louis Vuitton dress showing skin.

"I haven't heard from him in a few days, but I got him wrapped around my finger. He gonna be easy."

"I already know. We running circles around these lame niggas," Foxy added.

"How come you single, girl?" Rika asked Foxy.

"I ain't got time for love or to play games wit none of these busters. Plus, I ain't got time for a clown nigga to burn me or curse me with herpes," Foxy said laughing but serious.

"You right. I don't trust no nigga," Rika says.

"Shit, I don't trust a soul," Foxy said

"Cheers to that," Beth cut in, thinking about her next move for Lil Jet.

CHAPTER 17
UPTOWN, PHILLY

Sosa rented out a lounge for the Sosa Gang and the D.C. Crew meeting today. Everybody came out to take a seat at the long table. The D.C. Crew sat on one side and Sosa Gang sat on the other side. Everyone was quiet.

"Thanks for coming out. Everybody looking like money," Sosa stated, making a few niggas smile.

"This is a big day, gentlemen. We never had a meeting with the D.C. Crew and our gang, so I think we making history today," Twin stated.

"Facts, young bull," Kaba said sitting next to Wayne who didn't say a word yet.

Both sides could feel the tension between Lez and Wayne. It was so thick a person could cut it with a butter knife.

"Let's get started because I like to be short and brief," says Sosa.

"Shit, since when? Nigga, once you get going, your ass don't stop talking," Lil Hak joked, even making Wayne laugh. Loosen him up a little.

"Fuck you, nigga ... Now, back to what I was trying to say. Since we teamed up, shit had been crazy. Money has been coming in nonstop, but when the paper comes, the problems follow up. That's where we are right now, bro." Sosa looked around as he talked to see he had everyone's attention.

"I've had one for a while and I wanna know how this nigga Gee took over my hood," Lil Hak asked.

"To be real, I don't know, Lil Hak. One day I hear he came home, then the next thing I hear is he down with the ops," says Sosa, not really caring for the Gee situation because he crossed the gang and he didn't respect that.

"Maybe he found out we killed his sister by mistake," Twin said, thinking back to when he killed Dawgy and hit Gee's sister by accident.

"Shit happens, cuz," Kaba stated, already knowing the story.

"You want your block back? Take it then, bro. We not wasting time on that," Sosa told Lil Hak.

"Iight." Lil Hak hid his anger.

"Businesswise, I had a bad load a few weeks ago, but it's back to normal now, so no worries. Trust me. I want us all to focus on locking down these blocks, but these Outlaw niggas are trying to take over a few blocks of ours, so we have to hold on tight and wipe them out their own hoods," Sosa suggested.

"We also have a new problem in west Philly," Lez said.

"That's your area, right?" Wayne asked

"Like I was saying. There is a new group of women out there killing and getting money, and I think they gonna become an issue," Lez added.

"Before that happens, you and Wayne handle them. I'm sure the both of you can," Sosa said.

"Kill the bitches, not each other," Lil Jet joked, but everybody just looked at him, hoping he would shut up.

"Lez, you said this Kane nigga killed your brother?" Twin asked.

"Yeah," Lez shot back.

"Did you get any info on dude yet?" Kaba asked.

"I know who he is," Wayne cut in as the crew all looked at Wayne.

"Enlighten us, bull," Sosa said.

"I used to cop from him until I got arrested and found out he ratted on me," Wayne said.

"He was in the whole time. How could you work for him?" Lil Hak said, referring to OG Kane.

"Kane was making big moves from the jails. I met him in jail, and when I touched down, he was getting them things to me. A lot of shit. This is around the same time my crew was going at it with y'all. When I got arrested, I told Kane what happened in a letter because I trusted him, and he told the police everything for a time cut," Wayne said.

"So, we beefin' wit a gangsta rat," Twin added.

"Yep," Kaba says.

"We need to get him off the streets." Sosa paused, thinking.

"There are more Outlaw niggas that have high rankings just like him, and we don't even know who they are. For all we know, they can be sitting here, so we should go about this in a serious, smart way. Them dudes move like the Mob," Wayne told them all.

"You know a lot about dem cats," Lil Jet stated.

"I study my op, young bull. I advise you to do the same," Wayne shot back.

"We have another small problem that I will take care of, but I just want to let you know. There is a cop chick snooping around, trying to nail us, but I got a plan for her, so I'ma do my part and I hope all of you take care of y'all issues as well. Anybody got anything to say before I close out?" Sosa asked, thinking about how Karlee would've been waiting outside for him if she was still alive. Karlee would pop in his mind at the oddest times of the day. He needed to get her out of his mind. Sosa's sister told him he should start dating again, but he knew it was too soon. Nobody said a word, so he knew everything he stated today was signed and sealed. "Wayne and Lez, I need you to stay for a while," Sosa says, seeing the crazy look on their faces. Everybody got up to leave except them.

**

Lez couldn't believe Sosa just pulled that move on him.

"I see you still holding on to some dumb shit," Wayne spoke up.

"The dumb shit you started."

"You tried to kill me."

"Shit, bull, you did the same shit I did if not worst," Lez added.

"That shit behind me now. I'm on money."

"Me, too. So, we good?" Lez asked.

"Yeah, that shit behind me, bro," Wayne said as they embraced each other.

**

CONVENTION CENTER, PHILLY

There was a big concert today at the Convention Center and all the hottest singers and rappers came out to perform a Stop the Violence show. Meek Millz and Gilly Da Kid came out to show love and give a few good words of encouragement. Zarhya and a gang of her college buddies came to enjoy the night.

"This shit is crazy," Jameek said, looking around at all the people who came out. Jameek was one of Zarhya's good friends she met in school.

"Hell yeah, bitch," Zarhya says, looking at all the people scream and shout in her ear, and nine times out of ten they were the ones out in these streets killing. Zarhya was waiting on her boyfriend because he told her to meet him there.

"Aye, babe," a male voice said, creeping up behind her.

Zarhya turned around, smiling, already knowing the voice. "Hi, baby. I missed you," she said kissing Rizzy who rolled up with the dudes from the block. All Zarhya's friends had the look of envy and jealousy on their faces.

"You having fun," Rizzy asked, looking her up and down, licking his lips at how good she looked.

"Now, I am," she contested, blushing. Every time Rizzy came around, she would blush and get shy. They shared something so strong. People saw the chemistry from the outside. They ended up going out to eat, then Zarhya had to go back to school, but she told him next time she wanted some dick.

CHAPTER 18
SOUTHWEST, PHILLY

"Them niggas got me fucked up. I used to run this shit. I'm da reason why the body count went up over here. Niggas think I'ma just let some lame ass north Philly take my block, bull? Fuck nah, bro. Just because I was gone don't mean I wasn't coming back for mine. I don't like that nigga Gee anyway. The bull always had been a sucker." Lil Hak talked out loud, thinking Kaba was listening, but he was in the passenger's seat asleep.

Lil Hak and Kaba came out early to catch Gee and a crew of Outlaw niggas playing a game of basketball in the project's basketball court.

"What's you saying?" Kaba woke up. Last night he didn't get any sleep. He and a few of his boys from the D.C. Crew went out to Delaware to have a good time at a party.

"Nothing." Lil Hak shook his head, watching Gee dunk the basketball.

"Damn, he nice." Kaba watched Gee do his thing on the court.

When Lil Hak saw Gee sit down, it was time for him to bring his move. The only problem was all the niggas outside. Lil Hak knew mostly everybody outside on the court was an Outlaw member, and if they weren't, he knew they could run or duck. "Now," Lil Hak said, hopping out with an AR-15 assault rifle.

***

Gee was taking a break from the game to get his wind after playing five full court basketball games this morning. Everything had been perfect. He copped a new car, and the holidays were near so he planned to take his girl on a trip and spoil her. Gee moved her out of Oxford Circle into a nice crib and brought her a new car for being a ride or die bitch.

Max had been doing the right thing and now he was making over twenty thousand a day off of hand to hand. With a bunch of workers, Gee had to do payrolls, keep up with the re-up money, and dividing the product. The other day, Gee met OG Kane and he told

Gee how good of a job he had been doing in Larchwood. OG Kane also told him he wanted to give him another hood to control and Gee was down.

Hearing Sosa's gang name ring out through the city all day and Gee was fed up. He wanted bloodshed for his sister's death. Now he had his money and shooters up, and it was time to put his plan together.

It got a little chilly outside because winter was near, so Gee put on his sweatsuit. That's when the gunfire popped off and two of his workers went down.

Tat... Tat... Tat... Tat... Tat... Tat... Tat... Tat... Tat... Tat... Tat...

Gee raced to his gym bag to his left while ducking bullets to get him 9-millimeter FN handgun out. Seeing Lil Hak's bare face and some other nigga, he knew the gunmen were down with Sosa Gang.

Boc... Boc... Boc... Boc...

Gee hit the man shooting with Lil Hak in the forearm while Lil Hak hit two more of his goons. Niggas tried to run out of every gate entrance but Lil Hak was clipping everything in his path.

Tat... Tat... Tat... Boc... Boc...

Kaba fired toward Gee who was duck-walking, firing back with his left hand. Kaba's left forearm couldn't stop bleeding. He had to go. Not trying to die, he gave Lil Hak a look, letting him know it was time to go. Gee managed to get out of the war zone, so Lil Hak and Kaba left, almost tripping over dead bodies. Lil Hak was pissed off Gee made it out alive. He blamed Kaba's lack of awareness. There would be another time and Lil Hak knew that, but he was glad the message got through.

***

SOUTH PHILLY

The new strip club Champagne had beautiful, exotic dancers, bartenders, and bottle girls. Lez took Sosa out tonight because he knew Sosa had been under a lot of pressure since dealing with this Outlaw shit. To make matters worse, the death of Karlee took a lot out of him, so he wanted to bring him on a night on the town.

"That bartender bitch just gave me her number, talking about call her later. She want to rock my work." Sosa laughed, looking at the name and number on the napkin.

"What's her name?"

"Parie, or some dumb shit."

"You need some pussy. Fuck her before I do." Lez laughed.

"Nigga, you dumb. But, ayo, you saw that shit on the news?"

"In Larchwood?" Lez asked.

"Yeah. I think it was Lil Hak and his boy about Gee."

"Fuck do I know? The bull going crazy about da shit," Lez contested.

"Who dem niggas?" Sosa saw a group of dudes and bad bitches walk in the club.

"That little bitch," Lez said, making eye contact with the woman leading the pack, rocking a mink coat in a gold dress and heels to match.

"You know her?" Sosa couldn't really see who the chick was, but she looked like she was a celebrity or something.

"Nigga, that's Foxy, and she coming over here," Lez said, not in the mood for her dumb shit.

"Lez and Sosa, care if I join y'all? It's had been a while. We used to kick it all the time," Fox said, inviting herself to a seat, seeing a bottle girl come up to Lez.

"Can I get you another bottle," the thick redbone chick with tatts all over her thigh asked.

Before Lez could respond, Foxy answered, "Bitch, get the fuck away from here." Foxy gave the bottle girl an evil look and she took off.

"Foxy, you look nice. How you had been?" Sosa asked.

"Better than you. Sorry to hear about your girl," Foxy shot back, seeing the surprised look on his face.

"What the fuck do you want?" Lez asked.

"I think I'ma be honest with you both. There is something that you don't know about me, and I hate secrets, so I'ma tell you both. Since y'all killed my brother, I had been coming for your crew; especially Twin. To sum it all up, I'm an active leader of the Outlaws, and to be honest, I'm y'all least worry. Y'all have bigger worries than me and my bitches. The war is just started. Y'all chose the wrong side and fucked with the wrong bitch. After tonight, there is no more talking." She looked directly at Lez before she got up to leave, brushing past Lez, then she stopped and walked up to Lez and kissed his lips before slapping the shit out of him.

Sosa couldn't believe his ears. Never in a million years would he imagine Lez's ex-girl to be an op. Lez's mind raced. It was all starting to make sense now. Gunshots could be heard outside and Lez had five goons parked out front, so they rushed outside.

"Fuck," Sosa stated, seeing the two trucks filled with goons were host up and only one soldier was still breathing as people ran out the club, calling the police.

Lez's blood was boiling. He never had been so pissed off.

CHAPTER 19
YORK, PA

Two hours away from Philly was a small-town called York and Vera spent a lot of years there growing up, but she also spent some of her childhood in Miami, Florida where she was born. Even though Philly raised her, Vera still knew how to move around and blend in with the best of them.

Five years ago, she opened her own real estate company in York. She became so successful she opened a real estate company in Philly also. Today, Vera had two clients trying to close on two homes. One was already closed, and she was now showing around a white married couple.

She was guiding the couple through hardwood floors, four rooms upstairs and downstairs, large backyard, two car garage and it was located in a nice neighborhood close to a middle school.

After this, Vera had to go check on her 18-year-old son who lived a few blocks away with her sister. She was the mother of two beautiful children and played a big role in their lives. The only problem was that her husband Kane didn't know about the son she had while he was in prison. She did everything she could for Kane when he was in prison, but one thing she couldn't do was be a born-again virgin for him.

Vera was a Cuban woman, but she disliked Cuban men because they were all the same— self-centered and controlling. Coming to Philly, there were a lot of blacks and she got hooked. She loved the way African Americans' bodies looked, their swag, attitude, how they treated her, and she loved how a lot of them were blessed with large penises.

Her children were mixed. She felt like she betrayed Kane by having a baby on him with a man she knew long before him.

"Do y'all like it?" Vera asked the couple, stepping into the backyard.

"Yes, we love it, but can you give me and my husband a day or so to make a decision?" the chubby woman asked while holding her husband's hand.

"Sure, why not?"

"Thank you. I'm sure my wife is going to want it," the husband added.

"Let's hope so," Vera replied, smiling as she shook their hands. It was cold out today. She rocked her fur coat and brought out her Range Rover. She had to rush to her son's high school for his basketball game.

***

Prince ran up and down the court, making basket after basket. He was the school's star player in his senior year of high school. He just happened to see his mom walk into the gym, late as always, but he was glad she made it out. Prince was a handsome eighteen-year-old on his way to college, so many schools wanted him. All Division 1 colleges like Texas A&M, Alabama State, Miami University, UCLA, SC, Duke. He made the top twenty in the country's list at number nine.

Vera was so proud of her baby boy, but she really had her sister Givilana to thank for the help because Vera lacked in a lot of areas and motherhood was one. Having to raise another child in another city was hard but Vera tried her best to juggle work, marriage, and motherhood. One day she knew Prince would want to know who his dad was and Vera had no choice but to keep it real. Growing up she used to tell Prince his dad was a drug addict which is the best lie that hit her mind at the moment.

When the game ended Prince ran up to his mom and aunt, giving them hugs. Every male in the gym stared at Vera sexually because she looked twenty and badder than any bitch there. The only person who looked anywhere close to as good was Vera's sister who was dark, slim, pretty, short hair and alluring to look at. Prince hated he had a beautiful mom and aunt because people would stare and say slick shit when they came around.

"You made it," Prince said.

"Why wouldn't I?" Vera stated, wiping her lipstick off his cheek.

"Just saying," he stated.

"You want to go eat?" Vera asked.

"Yeah. I want to hear your opinion on these colleges. Let me get my stuff." Prince left.

"That boy loves you," Givilana said, seeing Prince runoff.

"He loves you, too," Vera joked.

"That boy better. Anyway, how's life in Philly? I ain't see you in a few days." Givilana disliked her sister hiding the fact that she had a son to her husband. Vera didn't even tell Prince he had a sister because she didn't want her daughter to tell her dad about Prince.

"I'm sorry. I got caught up," Vera told her.

"I bet, but you need to tell him," Givilana said before walking off, shaking her head.

***

SOUTH, PHILLY

Twin had just gotten done making his salat— a prayer for Muslims— in the mosque his dad ran. With his dad being an Imam, a Muslim leader, Twin didn't like coming around because he knew his dad would speak his mind.

"Do you know why we pray as Muslims?" Twin's dad came out the back of the Mosque.

"Yeah."

"Why?"

"To get closer to Allah," Twin contested.

"That's a main reason, but another one is our sins are forgiven. Everything we done and repented for before that prayer will be forgiven, but here is my question."

Twin knew his dad always had a twist and turn on whatever he said. Everything his dad said had meaning to it; that's why Twin always listened.

"Why be forgiven to continue to do the same thing? Was your repentance ever sincere or genuine? Ask yourself this, son. You already lost a sister, I lost a daughter. How many more lives will die at the palm of your hands?" Twin's dad walked off, heading in the same direction he came.

Twin had some food for thought as he let what his dad just said soak in.

***

GERMANTOWN, PHILLY

Sosa tailed the DEA lady. He had been busy trying to see what she had going on because he wasn't about to let her take him or his gang down. He followed her into a Taco Bell parking lot but he parked a few cars down, trying to lay low so she wouldn't see him.

"Can't be."

Sosa saw her exit the undercover car and walk right up to his window and knock. He rolled down his window feeling like a creep.

"Next time you follow someone, keep a distance, and don't flash your headlights." She laughed.

"You still trying to nail me?" Sosa asked.

"Maybe."

"You look nice," Sosa said, seeing how good she looked in her regular business suit with her hair done up.

"Come have lunch since you stalking a bitch anyway."

"I don't eat wit cops."

"But you stalk them. Sounds weird, but I'm going to eat. Keep an eye on the ride for me." She laughed, walking off.

Sosa felt dumb. He pulled off feeling like an ass, but he was starting to think of a better plan to handle her.

CHAPTER 20
NORTH PHILLY

Lil Jet drove the old Chevy through Badlands, following their target which was a new Porsche speeding through the main streets.

"How you get the drop on this nigga, though?" Twin asked from the passenger seat.

"This clown little brother goes to the same school as my niece." Lil Jet stopped at the red light behind six cars.

"How did you find that out?"

"One day I had to pick her up and as she talking about some dumb shit. I see this nigga Max come out with a little nigga who look just like him. Then my niece told me that's his big brother. He came to pick him up every day and he even gave her a ride once." Lil Jet knew today Max would be a goner at any cost.

"This nigga will be one less problem, I tell you. But I see you had been busy lately with a little redbone vibe." Twin saw a smile appear on his boy face.

"Yeah, at first me and ole girl was just on some sex shit, then thing got real, quick."

"Just stay focused, bro. A bitch will knock you off your square and they not meant to be trusted, especially a lot of these broads out here in the streets. You need to go snatch you up one of them classy rich chicks who got a bag," Twin suggests.

"Man, I love me a hood chick, bro."

"That's your problem now," Twin stated seeing, Max pull into the packed high school parking lot.

***

Max parked on the side of two school buses and waited on his little brother Ray to come out of school. Every day he picked up Ray from school. He loved his little brother. Since he was a kid Max basically raised him since there father wasn't there. He made sure he kept Ray in the flyest gear and gave him whatever he wanted and needed. Whenever Ray received good grades in school, Max would give him $5,000 to $10,000 in cash.

Ray knew Max's lifestyle but never once questioned him or what he was doing in the streets.

Since placing Gee in Larchwood, money had been at the highest peak it's ever been for the crew since opening shop in Lil Hak's old projects, but it was fair game. There was no doubt in his mind that a war over Larchwood would spark soon; bigger than what it already was.

He saw his little brother rush out of school with his backpack with two girls chasing him. Max laughed, knowing his brother was a young pimp nigga, fucking all the little high school bitches. "You still got them chasing you, I see," Max says when Ray hopped in the car out of breath.

"I fucked both of them with the same condom last week," Ray stated laughing, putting on his seatbelt.

"You about to have one of these hoochie mamas pregnant." Max pulled off in his Porsche, unaware of the car tailing him.

Stopping at a stop sign, a car pulled up to the side of him and opened fire.

Bloc... Bloc... Bloc... Bloc...

Max he popped out firing at the ops. He saw Lil Jet and Twin leaning out their windows.

Bloc... Bloc... Bloc... Bloc...

"Shit!" Max yelled seeing bullets hit Ray in his upper chest and neck.

Bloc... Bloc... Bloc... Bloc...

Both cars engage in a gun battle before buses sped by them, hitting the rear of Lil Jet's car.

Max got back in his Porsche, almost getting hit by the speeding school bus. Looking to his left he saw Ray slumped in the passenger seat dead. Tears rolled out his eyes. Hearing police sirens, he put the car in drive, racing off so he could bring the body to his aunty who was a licensed nurse but was retired at home.

***

LOVE PARK, PHILLY

Sosa drove past Love Park and put his car to a halt when he saw the familiar woman at a photo shoot. He immediately pulled over and double parked next to a van before climbing out. Today he was going to get her because the woman hadn't left his mind since Sosa first laid eyes on her at the airport. When the woman told him her social media site, he forgot it once he got into his conversation with Barry that day, but he never forgot how beautiful she looked. There were very few people's names Sosa could remember, but he could never forget Allure.

Since losing Karlee, women had been in a 3D vision to him, but Allure caught his attention the same way Karlee did when he first laid eyes on her.

Sosa had on a nice Versace sweatsuit with a hoodie attached to it because wintertime in Philly was no joke. Walking closer to the group of people taking pictures of Allure standing next to a big rock, he figured she had to be famous, an entertainer, model, or some other well-known public figure because she liked it but it looked too professional for her own personal use.

Seeing Allure smile, pose, and have fun in front of the camera made him see how much of a natural poser she was as if Allure had been doing this since a baby. When the photo shoot was over Allure spoke to a few people while looking over her flicks, liking all of them. Allure saw Sosa and did a double look at him before walking to him. She recognized him from airport that day she came back to Philly after a photo shoot in Miami. "Hey, you. don't I remember you?" she asked, covering her body with a Louis Vuitton coat.

"I hope you do! Ms. Allure."

"Okay, you know my name. Good memory, Sosa." She blushed.

"What you got going on here?" Sosa looked at all the people standing around.

"Oh, I model. This shoot is for a magazine heavy overseas, and I have another one in two hours in Camden, New Jersey. You should come," she suggested.

"Me?"

"No, the other you." She laughed at his dumb remark.

"Okay. I'm not doing nothing anyway," Sosa lied. He had to meet Wayne but he could call and put it off until tomorrow.

"Great. I get sick of being around all these promoters, managers, and creeps."

"You're their investment."

"I'm my own investment. They need me." Allure pointed to her chest.

Sosa never saw such a beautiful smile like Allure had. She was the truth and he felt the connection.

CHAPTER 21
WEST PHILLY

Beth recently got her own two-bedroom apartment near the Wynnefield area in the cut. She lived in a dead-end area by herself. Beth didn't even tell her sister Rika where she lived ye. The only person who knew was Lil Jet.

Her relationship with Lil Jet was getting real serious. Last night he opened up to her and admitted at first it was just a sex thing, but when he got to know her he got hooked. Lil Jet told Beth he loved her last night, and she froze up not knowing what to say or do.

This morning, Rika called and asked her how the homework was coming along which is code word for the Lil Jet mission. Beth told her Lil Jet was out of town still somewhere. Lying to Rika took a lot out of her but she knew Rika had a big mouth and wouldn't hesitate to run straight to Foxy and tell her shit.

Beth sat on her bed, unable to breathe as she took deep inhales thinking about the news she just found out. After taking her second pregnancy test, Beth is pregnant and she couldn't believe it. The only person she had been having any type of sexual relationships with in past few months is Lil Jet. Being pregnant was a big shock. She was confused and having mixed feelings because Beth felt like she loved Lil Jet, too.

***

WEST PHILLY

Rika and a few chicks open a trap house in a hood called Da Bottom on 39th and Mount Vernon. The small block they were on wasn't compared to 38th and Aspin where Sosa Gang niggas had shit doing big numbers. Four girls on the block looking cute with two chicks in the building pitching to the feins didn't look suspect so they had a good thing going. Every now and then a few dudes would pull up and spit game to the women who looked more delighted to listen.

Rika knew nobody would ever expect a bunch of sexy women selling a ton of drugs right down the street from the ops. Foxy told her the beef was lit with them and the Sosa Gang so Rika had Dracos and Glocks with extendos attached to all of them just in case they pulled up.

Selling right under Sosa Gang's nose felt good to Rika. The feeling of power never hit her so hard.

Beth had been acting weird since Foxy sent her to Lil Jet and Rika didn't like it at all because that wasn't like her sister to push her away. She planned to lock into it soon, maybe sometime this weekend.

"Girl, I'm sick of these clown ass niggas trying to bag me wit they weak ass game," Aaliyha said, walking away from some young nigga who tried to spit his mack, but Aaliyha gave him a fake number and sent him on his way.

"It's getting late. I have to go pick my baby up from the nanny," Simona said, getting her purse off the trunk of an old Chevy.

"You need a ride?" Rika stated before turning around facing Simona which was bad timing.

Aaliyha saw men came from left and right with guns at a fast pace.

"Rika!" shouted Aaliyha, going for the Draco inside the trash can, letting off shots first.

Tat… Tat… Tat… Tat…

Aaliyha hit two shooters before bullets ate her back out, killing her. The shooters put holes in Aaliyha like she was target practice. Rika was the only one who had a gun on her hip and she pulled it out, letting her Glock bark.

Bloc… Bloc… Bloc… Bloc… Bloc… Bloc…

Simone tried to run which turned out to be bad for her. Twin fired six rounds in Simona's stomach, trying to get closer to Rika, but she was moving like a soldier. Rika popped two more of Twin's shooters back-to-back before running across the street.

The rest of Rika's crew took off rushing into the building for safety. Rika had to save herself as she got away from the gunmen trying to knock her head off.

***

CHAESTA, PA

Zarhya had a date night with Rizzy and he took her to one of the most expensive restaurants around the Philly area.

"You did it up tonight. I'm very impressed," Zarhya said looking around.

"I had to do it on a boss level. Shit, you wasn't trying let me take you out," Rizzy said eating his meal.

"I'm very boujee."

"Oh, fo'sho. I see that now," Rizzy joked.

"Since we been vibing, I feel special, but there are a few question marks I have." Zarhya's statement made him move around in his chair.

"I'm listening."

"Your lifestyle isn't something I look for in a man." She was upfront.

"You had been knew I was in the field, living this type of life." Rizzy stopped eating so she could see how serious he was.

"I know, but what if you go to jail or something happens?"

"Then be there for a nigga."

"I'm not built to do a bid." She didn't hesitate to be honest.

"So, you not fully a ride or die type. Shit, I thought you was, or at least you portrayed to be," he told her.

"What? I'm a real bitch just because I'm not trying waste my life doing a thirty or twenty year bid with a nigga and I don't even know what's in his heart?" she suggested.

"I don't know what to tell you, sweetheart. This is me."

"I understand that, but I know you can do better and want more for yourself than the streets. My pops and brother live a street life, and I'm sick of seeing people close to me give their soul to the streets." She got emotional thinking about Barry and Sosa.

Rizzy never heard her talk about family members so he felt like the two were closer. He really liked Zarhya and her character was strong for such a young woman. She had her head on right. "How about this? We enjoy each other company and not worry about what the future holds."

"We can't hide from the future."

"I'm not trying to at all, I'm just planning for today."

"I can get wit that," Zarhya says, eating her delicious food.

"Now that's out the way, can I get a taste of that thing later?" He licked his juicy lips.

"Of this?" She lifted up some food off her plate.

"Nah. I'm talking about the real deal, boo."

"Maybe in your dreams."

"Damn. How long you finna have me on this shit?" Rizzy wanted to fuck her so bad.

"Whenever I think you're ready. And trust me, you will drown before you even get in this pool," she joked.

"You pop a lot of shit."

"Do I?"

"Girl, you're a mess. Let's eat and go watch the stars in the sky."

"Now, that's third base action." She made him crack up.

CHAPTER 22
SOUTH PHILLY

Barry took Elina to Shyne Jewelry store so he could ice her out and he had a good relationship with the owner who was from the Middle East. While Barry and the owner talked about some other business in the back, Elina was going crazy.

"What's this?" Elina asked an employee who had been helping her pick out the hottest new shit.

"This here is a GIA certified round diamond stud with VSI clarity," the white man said looking at the way her titties fit perfectly in her dress top.

"How many carrots?" Elina wanted to know.

"I believe twenty-four."

"Oh, how about this one?" Elina pointed at another bracelet.

"Okay. Now, we're talking. This is a white gold emerald bracelet, weighing at eighteen-point-nine, thirteen-point-six millimeter width, and the length is seven-point-five inches," he told her, seeing that it caught her eye.

"Those earrings next to it goes with it?" She asked.

"Yes, and the ring which is eighteen karats of white gold with a one-point-eighty-eight diamond with eleven-point-seven in the center. This collection is a special edition. It's very rare." The employee knew the bracelet, ring, and earrings would look stunning on her.

"What's the price on all of this?" Elina liked what she saw.

"All this will come out to a hundred and fifty-five thousand, but I'm the first to tell you it's worth it," he convinced her.

"I'll take it." She looked to Barry to see him shaking hands with the owner as if they'd just come to a business agreement.

"You ready, babe?" Barry came behind her, holding on to her curvy hips, looking over her shoulder at the nice, shiny jewelry laid out in front of her. Barry had a closet full of jewelry, so this didn't impress him. He just wanted to ice her out.

"I want this." Elina pointed at the collection in front of her.

"Okay, cool. Ring it up," Barry told the employee.

"Yes, sir." The employee rushed to do as asked.

"Thank you, babe."

"Let's go to dinner now," he suggested, hoping to spend time with his girl today.

"How's about we skip dinner and I eat that dick," she whispered into his car.

"Well, if you suggest, my dear," Barry replied, ready for the long night he had in store because Elina could fuck and suck all night.

***

NORTHEAST PHILLY

Mrs. Ford watched the interaction with Sosa and Lez. She ran Lez's license plate into her computer and his face popped up with a few tickets and dumb shit; nothing serious. When seeing his nickname "Lez" she knew who he was. Lez was one of the top dawgs for Sosa Gang. His name had been popping up for a while now more than anybody in the crew besides Lil Hak.

Staring at Lez, she found him very attractive; way more than Sosa. There was something about Lez that made her body tense. Maybe it was his style, or height, or good looks she found handsome.

Seeing Sosa get in his car and leave she wanted to play a little game because Mrs. Ford was sure Lez already knew a DEA agent was on their line.

When Lez climbed in his car inside the parking lot of a nursing home she raced into the lot with her red and blue lights flashing. The look she saw on Lez's face was to pull off and run, but when he laid eyes on her that shit changed.

Mrs. Ford jumped out with her gun cocked as if she was ready to blow his face off or something. "Get out the car with your hands up, now," Ms. Ford shouted.

"Damn it. I ain't even do shit," says Lez, climbing out his car with his hands up.

Ms. Ford got closer to him and told him to turn around and face the car. "What do you have on you?" she demanded.

"A wallet."

"That's all?"

"No. I got a bomb in my pocket. What the fuck it look like?" Lez got an attitude with her while being frisked.

"You got a big mouth." Ms. Ford was now done patting him down to find nothing but a wallet.

"What, lady? I was minding my business before you came and fucked up my day," Lez stated as she turned him around.

"Who was you just talking to a second ago?" she asked.

Lez paused for a second, lost in her beauty. There was no denying how attractive she was.

"Are you deaf?" she yelled, waving her hand in front of his face, seeing he was zoned out.

"Lady—"

"The name is Mrs. Ford," she cut him off.

"Mrs. Ford, this is racial profiling." He made her laugh.

"I'm black, too."

"Well, you can be black and still be racist."

"That sounds dumb ass fuck," she contested, never had been called a racist.

"Whatever you want to know, Mrs. Ford, I'ma be the first to tell you I'm not the one to ask."

"You think your friends gonna save you when it's all over?" She questioned him.

"It's not about them, Mrs. Ford. In life, a person has to own up to their part and stand on what they believe in. You feel me?" Lez saw her eyes soften.

"So, you fear Sosa or something? You really think if they offer him two hundred years he wouldn't give you up?"

Lez laughed and shook his head, staring her down like she lost it. "I don't know a Sosa. Never heard of him, Mrs. Ford. You have the wrong person, I believe." Lez matched her smirk.

"That's fair, Lez, but let me tell you something."

"Before you go on, Mrs. Ford, please get that booger out your nose. It's been bothering me for the longest," Lez told her as she rushed to her work car to get some tissue, feeling embarrassed. Lez was starting to enjoy this conversation with her. Sosa told him about Mrs. Ford a few times. He had been waiting on her to make an appearance. Before Sosa pulled off minutes ago, he let Lez know Mrs. Ford was parked across the street watching them.

"Sorry about that. But as I was saying… Well, I forgot what I was about to say so you lucky. I'ma be watching you." She turned to walk off.

"Mrs. Ford, I would love for a beautiful woman such as yourself to watch me," Lez told her.

"Don't push it." Mrs. Ford tried to hold her blush because she wasn't used to getting such good compliments from anybody. She always had on a serious face, trying to play hard because deep down she was soft.

***

SOUTH PHILLY

Lil Jet and one of his female cousins were in a big body Benz, blasting rap music on his way to his crib so he could pick up some money to take her shopping for the baby shower. Seeing his little cousin pregnant about to pop made him want a baby himself, but he knew the life of a gangsta would soon catch up to him. So, having a kid right now wasn't on his bucket list.

"You coming to the baby shower, cuz?" she asked, rubbing her big belly.

"Of course. You my favorite little cousin."

"So, you not mad at me?"

"Nah. I understand, but you gotta get your mind right and provide. It's hard out here, Nana."

"I know, Kevin." She called Lil Jet by his real name.

When he pulled up to his apartment building, Beth's car was parked in the front. He didn't expect to see her there, but it must've been good timing because he wanted to introduce her to Nana.

Getting out the car he saw Beth fly out her new Lexus LC coupe like superwoman.

"You nasty, nigga. So, you bring bitches here, huh?" Beth jumped up in is face, getting loud and ratchet outside as people walked up and down the block.

"Calm down."

"Nigga, fuck you. I can't believe I let you foul me, Kevin. You're a dog just like the rest of them. I hate you," she shouted in tears.

Lil Jet could tell she really did care for him. Now and it made him care for her a lot more.

"Beth, that's my little cousin Nana I told you about who was pregnant." Lil Jet saw her tears.

She looked at him and Nana feeling crazy. "I'm sorry, Kevin. I thought…" She felt so dumb. Beth couldn't even get her words out.

"It's straight, babe. I'm not even tripping. But just know I won't play you, bae. I really care and love you." Lil Jet's words were genuine, and this was the first time she felt it in her heart.

"I love you, too, Kevin."

"This is your first time saying that, so I believe you."

"Because I don't play with love."

"Neither do I," Lil Jet added.

"So, I guess this news will really show how much you love me. I'm pregnant, Kevin." Beth didn't see any signs on his face and her heart started to race at a rapid speed of fear. When she saw him shed a tear of joy and a big smile appeared on Lil Jet's face, she hugged him.

"Oh my God, baby, I wasn't ready for this, but you're the only woman I would ever want to have a baby with," he told her as Nana approached them.

"Hey, I'm Nana."

"I'm Beth."

"She pregnant, cuz. We about to have some bad ass babies around here," Lil Jet joked

"That's great," Nana said admiring how pretty Beth was and how they looked good together.

All three of them went out shopping and enjoyed the winter day. It was a few days before Christmas, so the city was full of good vibes.

CHAPTER 23
NORTHEAST PHILLY

Today was Christmas Eve and the city had red and green lights all over the place, giving the city a good feel. Plus, heavy snow outside gave the day a Christmas Eve vibe.

Kaba was a born Muslim, so he didn't celebrate holidays beside Ramadan, but his girlfriend Mehya was a devoted Christian, so he came out to pick up a few gifts for her family with her.

"Thanks for coming out, daddy," Mehya said as they walked into Wal-Mart, brushing the snow off their coats.

"You lucky I'm feeling nice," he says.

"I'ma make it up to you," she said sexually.

"Right here? I'm down for that."

"Boy, you lost your dumb mind," she told him, hitting his arm. Mehya is a beautiful chocolate woman with a blessed body. Her booty was so fat she couldn't walk nowhere without getting harassed.

Kaba had been making big moves in North and West Philly while Wayne focused on South and Southwest. They went shopping for over an hour in the store and Kaba was ready to leave.

"You gonna help me wrap all this stuff up, babe," she asked, placing everything in the cart after the clerk ranged it all up.

"Hell nah."

"Oh, word?" She acted shocked, but Mehya knew Kaba was a devoted Muslim and she would never do nothing to disrespect his religion one bit.

"I'ma take you to my crib or your mom's house? I have to take care of something," Kaba stated, paying for the items before leaving the store.

"My mom's crib. Everybody getting ready for Christmas tomorrow," Mehya says as people continued to ambush the store for the holiday rush.

Getting closer to the car, two vans pulled up behind them. Kaba nor Mehya saw the movement until they heard the first round go off.

Tat… Tat… Tat… Tat…

Mehya caught a clean shot to the dome, knocking her off her feet, leaving her in a snow pile on her back, bleeding out the head. Kaba fired back at the van, hitting one of the shooters, but goons jumped out the other van.

Tat… Tat… Tat… Tat…

Bullets hit Kaba in his right thigh, dropping him. As soon as Kaba's body hit the ground, the goons snatched him up, tossing him in the van. It took four of them to get Kaba in the van as he was fighting them off the best he could.

***

SOMEWHERE IN PHILLY

Kaba's blindfold was finally taken off as he felt pain all through his body, not only from being shot but because his kidnappers dragged him downstairs and all across the floor. Looking around the dark room he couldn't really get a good look at the six people standing in front of him. He could tell the kidnappers had small body frames as if they were young boys or teens. "Where the fuck am I?" Kaba shouted, but his cries went unheard as the kidnappers just stood there.

"Kaba, welcome," a female voice says, walking down the stairs. Then he saw the basement lights come on.

"What the fuck is this shit? Y'all some bitches?" Kaba yelled, seeing all chicks dressed in black. He knew something was off because the kidnappers needed four people to get him in the van. They weren't strong at all, which made him think teenagers set this up.

"We're not bitches, we are Divas. Black beautiful women who are sick of niggas like you and your gang trying to disrespect us and treat us like we don't make the world go around. So, now, you look like the bitch." Foxy was face to face with him now.

Kaba had his hands and legs tied to a chair, stripped down to his boxers

"What the hell do you want? I don't even know who you are," Kaba told her.

"Oh, you finna find out today. I'm da bitch your crew wished they never fucked with. I'm a true Outlaw."

"Ain't no chicks in the Outlaws. Who set this shit up?" Kaba really thought this was a joke.

"Don't you know it's horrible to judge a book by its cover?"

"Fuck you and your book, bitch. Do what you finna do. I'm D.C. Crew for life."

"I hear that. I'm not doing shit to you, but guess who is? Tahiry!" Foxy yells as Kaba thought he was hearing shit because he had a sister named Tahiry.

Kaba saw his sister Tahiry approach him with a metal baseball bat with a serious look on her face. "Tahiry, what the fuck you doing? I'm your brother."

"Foxy is my only family," Tahiry said, looking over to Foxy, who smiled at the acknowledgement.

"You don't know this bitch." Kaba couldn't believe this.

Kaba and Tahiry had a good bond until she went off and started stripping in clubs to make a living while being homeless.

"When I was homeless, selling my pussy, you was riding around in luxury cars. But we family? No, never. Foxy made a way for me, not you, Kaba. So, you've been dead to me. Bet that."

Before Kaba could plead to his sister, she swung the bat to his skull. Tahiry continued to bash Kaba's head in with a bat over fifty times until chunks of brain noodles covered the floor. Foxy watched the whole thing, proud of her girl. She recruited women from all over to show them how to get money the right way.

Romell Tukes

CHAPTER 24
SHARON HILL, PHILLY

Roddy and Wayne chilled in a nice mini mansion Wayne had just bought for himself and Abby. His girlfriend had the house fixed up so nice it looked like they lived there a few years rather than a few weeks.

"Y'all hungry? I'm about to cook dinner," Abby asked them, entering the spacious living room area.

"Nah, we straight, sis," Roddy said, rolling his wheelchair to the mini bar to get a drink of liquor. Since coming out the hospital, he had been drinking all day and fucking dancers and Instagram models who were selling pussy. Lucky Roddy's manhood still worked, but everything else below that was finished; numb to feeling.

"Thanks, baby," Wayne told her, grabbing his baby girl to give her a kiss.

"We still going out tonight?" She asked Wayne.

"Yes."

"Oh, Roddy, my homegirl asked about you the other day." Abby saw Roddy's face light up because he had been trying to fuck a few of her friends for years, but they were all the stuck up type.

"Which one?" Roddy turned the wheelchair, giving her his full attention with a bottle of Henny in his lap.

"The big one. Rachel," Abby says, seeing Wayne laugh.

"Rachel … Hold on. You talking about the three hundred pound bitch who looks pregnant with twins?" Asked Roddy

"Don't talk about my friend like that, Roddy, she likes you. It's not about looks no more. You need to find a real woman." Abby sat in Wayne's lap.

"Hell nah. I'm good," Roddy contested.

"We gonna find a suga mama, then." Wayne made Abby laugh before she got up to leave to cook dinner so they could eat before going out to a lounge.

"Now she gone, cuz. I can't believe this nigga Kaba got caught up," Wane said, disappointed about his boy's death.

"They left his body on his grandmom porch, cuz. That's some next type shit, bro. Them Outlaw niggas out here doing the most." Roddy had a lot of love for Kaba, so his death sparked a big roar with in the D.C. Crew and they were ready the flip Philly upside down for him.

"The crew and Sosa Gang hurt by this, but we gotta stay focused and I need your help, bro," Wayne suggested.

"Anything." Roddy moved at attention because he missed the game.

"I want you to handle all money affairs and drug transactions Kaba and me was doing together, but I have to put my real attention on Kane," Wayne says.

"I can't believe Kane is home," Roddy stated, knowing the legend's name.

"He's about to be a dead man. I know that," Wayne stated, hearing Abby call his name.

"Facts," Roddy added, gulping the bottle of Henny happy to be back in the mix.

***

UPPER DARBY, PHILLY

Sosa rode through a nice middle-class section listening to Big Sean, liking the rapper's swag and lyrics. Tonight, he had a lunch date with Allure. They have had been seeing each other almost every day in the last two weeks. Allure reminded him so much of Karlee in a lot of ways, but he liked everything about her.

The death of Kaba had him pissed off because he really liked the young man. Kaba was smart, business-minded, and a real soldier. Sosa knew there is a big war right now, so he understood the tactics and the outcome. His dad needed to speak to him later, so after his time with Allure he had to go see his pops.

Stopping at a red light, nodding to the music, he didn't see the pick-up truck to his right.

Boc... Boc... Boc...

Sosa ducked as bullets busted his glass window before he raised with a Glock 27 with a 30-shot clip.

Bloc... Bloc... Bloc... Bloc... Bloc... Bloc...

Shooting back at the pick-up truck he was able to get a good look at the shooter before pulling off. The gunman was an old man Sosa never saw before. "What the fuck?" Sosa saw blood dripping down his arm, thinking he got hit up. Sosa realized a piece a window glass was stuck in his arm and it felt worse than a bullet. Sosa drove all the way down the street in a white neighborhood with a shot out window and bullet holes in his car. He pulled into a gas station and rushed inside.

"You got a first aid kit and tweezers?" Sosa asked the store clerk who was eating chips, not trying to be bothered.

When he saw Sosa bleeding everywhere, he jumped to attention. "Here you go. It's all back here." The man got everything Sosa requested plus a bottle of alcohol.

Sosa went in the bathroom and tried to get the glass out his arm with the tweezers, putting pressure on it, seeing a little of it come out at a time. "Fuck!" He cried, pulling out the glass. When it came out, blood poured out non-stop. He poured alcohol all over it. Feeling that burn almost made him cry. Sosa placed paper towels over it to hold the bleeding.

Allure was calling his phone. He answered and told her he had to reset their lunch because something came up and she sounded sadden. Sosa needed a new car and to change his Louis Vuitton suit he wore that was all red with bloodstains now.

***

UPTOWN, PHILLY

OG Kane exited his pick-up truck in the movie theater to meet his daughter Foxy so they could go over the next re-up agreement. He was a little surprised at how fast she had been moving the product, but he knew Foxy was the female virgin of him.

Catching Sosa lacking at the light he knew would be a once in a lifetime thing because Sosa moved like a ninja. Seeing the nice car at the light, Kane had no idea who was in it until he saw Sosa's face, then had to make his move. Missing Sosa had to be a miracle in disguise because Kane rarely missed his targets when he busted his gun at anybody.

Walking into the theater he saw Foxy standing next to a food station, rocking a sweatsuit, looking like a regular chick. "Hey, baby girl. How you been?" Kane gave her a light hug, feeling she wasn't really into it.

"What's going on?" Her reply was flat.

"Are you sure this is a good place to talk?"

"I got movie tickets to see this corny ass movie that nobody will be in." Foxy walked into theater six.

Kane really wanted to find out what Foxy's real problem was, but he didn't want to push her away. Not being there as a father would make any person feel abandoned and scared.

Inside the movie theater, it was dark and there were no more than six people inside. It was perfect.

"I have all the money for you outside," Foxy stated.

"You traveling with that much money on you isn't smart at all, Foxy."

"It's a little too late for you to play good father."

"This is business."

"Sure."

"You must be this hard, Foxy? I'm trying to set shit straight between us. Yes, I fucked up in the past, but you're my daughter. I'm really working to make shit right between us," Kane suggested.

"Don't waste your time. Let's just focus on this bag and the Outlaws. It's only four of us at the head table, Kane. If you haven't noticed, we at war. You're running around chasing a Cuban bitch, while me and mine are out here in the streets. We are on the front line for the team," she spoke with a stern tone.

"Let me tell you something, little girl. I shed blood, tears, and pain for this shit just so you can have a seat. I wanted to pass it on. I risked my life for this, so don't come talk to me about sacrifices. I put my all into this shit. If there was one thing your mother should've told you about me, is I earned honor and scars at the same time. This life is all I know, Foxy. I'm not regular and neither are you. Let's get to business or get the fuck out of your chair. Emotions and business don't mix," he told Foxy.

"You right. My girl got the money in a white Ford for you. Give me a location for the next pick up. I'ma handle everything on my end."

"Good. I'ma call you tomorrow. Tell your people to call Rizzy. He will meet them to pick up the paper. Do you got his number?"

"Yes."

"Call him." Kane got up to leave.

Foxy couldn't believe how her father just went in on her, but she had no choice but to respect it.

Once back outside, she called Rizzy, whom she hadn't met yet, only spoken to once before. Foxy told him her girls were coming to South Philly to meet him.

***

SOUTH PHILLY

Rizzy had a low key apartment near Sigel Street, where he stashed money at for Kane. Only Max, Kane, and him knew about this location in Building 79. Rizzy exited the building and walked across the street to another apartment building where he had an apartment. He used this building as a detour for jack boys.

A few minutes ago, Foxy called him and he was now waiting on her people to arrive.

Rizzy never saw Foxy, but he knew she was a leading member at the table. Kane revealed that there were two more leaders he knew nothing about.

There was a white Ford creeping down the block with two bad ass chicks in the front. Both women hopped out with phat asses, grabbing large Louis Vuitton and Gucci shopping bags out of the car.

"You Rizzy?" One of them asked.

"Yeah, come inside." Rizzy led the women inside to apartment 1D, which was his cooking house that he'd been using to cook coke and cut dope.

Once inside, the women placed everything on the floor.

"That's from Foxy."

"I know, thank you." Rizzy looked at both women, who smiled and walked out. They were talking about how they would fuck him.

Rizzy knew he could have pressed up on the women but he had something real going on with Zarhya. The love connection he shared with Zarhya was special. He knew good women were hard to come by, so he treated her like she was the last woman on earth.

Looking into all the bags, he saw money stacked up. Counting all that paper wasn't going to happen, with a money machine or not. He knew Max would move the money in a few hours, so he left the apartment.

***

"This nigga fucking dumb as shit, cuz," Lil Jet stated, watching Rizzy walk out of the building.

"You right but I really want to blow his brains out right now, cuz," Lez told Lil Jet.

"I got a question bro because I'm not understanding something."

"Everything ain't meant to be understood."

"I get that, but this is real because I don't know how you was fucking the opp." Lil Jet laughed, hearing about the chick who got a position in the Outlaws. This was all new to him.

"Look, he leaving. Let's run up in there." Lez skipped over his dumb question because he ain't feel like talking about Foxy. Especially, after the way she violated at the club a while back, killing his men outside.

"Fuck my question, huh?"

"Yep," Lez said, seeing a text from Sosa saying he almost got toasted but he good.

"My girl got her first doctor appointment tomorrow," Lil Jet stated before seeing Lez read a text and get mad.

"Sosa almost got wet up."

"Nah bull, that's crazy." Lil Jet could not believe it.

"He straight. Come on, let's slide up in here, playboy."

Lez and Lil Jet snuck into the apartment building where they saw Rizzy leave from, shutting off the light in apartment 1D. Lil Jet kicked in the front door with their guns out but not a single soul was in sight.

After five seconds of searching the apartment, they found the money and it was a lot of it.

"Damn, these niggas getting money," Lil Jet stated.

"Nigga they stealing our blocks."

"I guess you right, but them bitches who dropped off this money asses was OD phat."

"Who you telling?" Lez saw them too, but his focus was not on women.

Romell Tukes

CHAPTER 25
WEST PHILLY

Beth and Lil Jet waited in a nearby clinic to be seen by a doctor, who she planned to have during her whole pregnancy.

"You good babe?" Beth asked him, snapping him out of his trance.

"Yeah, facts. Why you ask?"

"Just checking, but thanks for coming. I be nervous and I know if I was to do this by myself, shit will be stressful," she admitted. She saw many single mothers struggling with children and being pregnant.

"You never got to worry about that, shawty. I won't turn on you. That's deadbeat, goofy shit. I'm not on that," he told her.

"That's sweet. Time will tell."

"How about we start today with me showing what type of man I am?"

"What the hell you talking, boy?" She asked, looking at him oddly.

"I brought us a condo, baby. I want us to move in together. I really love you and I'ma do anything to prove it." Lil Jet saw tears in her eyes.

"You better not be playing, boy." She wiped her face as the doctor came out and called her name.

"Never will I play with you."

"I'll kill your black ass if you do," she told him with a smile but very serious.

"Crimes of passion always turn me on," he joked.

"Boy, shut up. Come on, that's us." Beth loved everything about Lil Jet. She didn't tell her sister about her pregnancy because Rika thought she was still trying to set him up and so did Foxy.

Sooner or later, she knew she would have to face the truth with them both. The outcome could go anyway and that's what Beth really feared. She felt like she was torn between two lines.

***

NORTHEAST PHILLY
DAYS LATER

Max, Rizzy, Foxy and the two women who dropped off the money to Rizzy last week, were all brought in front of OG Kane in an abandoned church.

The day Rizzy collected the money and left it in the stash house, Max went by one hour later as he always did and transferred it across the street to the real stash house or he brought it to a Southwest stash spot.

OG Kane had five goons behind him ready to leave somebody dead. At Kane's head nod, they would kill everyone, including Foxy. Kane told them that was their fate if anybody moved wrong.

"Rizzy and Foxy, both of you were the last to see my money besides these two lovely females who work for you, Foxy," Kane said, walking in front of the church like a preacher at Sunday service.

"Yes, but my girls were told to do a certain thing and they did just that. After it left their hands, it became out of my hands," Foxy told all of them, letting them know she wasn't with no snake shit. She was a real ride or die Outlaw.

"Don't put that shit on me. Once they brought the money upstairs, I did as I always did and left the crib, locking the door and waiting for Max to text," Rizzy said.

"You left before or after Max texted you?" Kane asked, raising his eyebrow.

"After. I can't lie, I was in a rush," Rizzy shot back, looking at Foxy suck her teeth. He couldn't lie. She was a dime, and her pussy print was crazy in the purple tights she had on.

"Leaving eight hundred fifty thousand dollars, in a rush huh?" Kane said, laughing to himself.

"We did our part. We don't steal," one of Foxy workers said as Foxy gave her a look to shut up.

"I think it was them Sosa gang niggas," Max stated.

"Did I ask you Max because you should have been there to collect my money? Did you have a voice then?" Kane got in Max's face, upset.

"I fucked up," Max admitted because he was in some pussy when the spot got robbed.

"Can we go?" One of Foxy's friends asked as Kane looked at both women with a smile.

"Of course," Kane said, going into his lower back
Bloc... Bloc... Bloc... Bloc... Bloc... Bloc... Bloc... Bloc...
Kane killed both of Foxy workers. She ain't even flinch. She got upset because he went too far.

"Max and Rizzy, both of you owe me four hundred thousand dollar a piece. Foxy, you owe my fifty thousand dollars. All of you better have my fucking money in seven days or that's going to be y'all ass." Kane looked at the two women laying on the church carpet in a pool of blood that kept flowing. Kane walked out with his guards, ice grilling all of them.

Max, Rizzy, and Foxy shook their heads at each other as if one of them set the whole shit up, but they all knew who caused this problem.

CHAPTER 26
SOUTHWEST PHILLY

Gee felt like his life turned into a movie overnight since dealing with the Outlaws and taking over Larchwood projects. Almost every night, he was in a shootout with Sosa Gang or the D.C. Crew, who was turned up since Kaba's death.

Lil Hak had been trying his best to get his hood back, but Gee wasn't about to make it easy for him.

"Ayo, Gee!" A young nigga, who hustled for Gee, yelled out.

"Micro, what's the word, cuz?"

"You see that little lady over there coming out the building." Micro stated.

"Yeah, what about her?" Gee looked to his far left.

"That's Lil Hak's mom or something, I think."

"You think?"

"Well, I know. She used to babysit me. That's how I know him," Micro said before Gee walked off.

"Mrs." Gee approached the little lady from behind, seeing the older woman turn around to see who was calling.

***

Mrs. North was Lil Hak's auntie, who basically raised him. She was coming from visiting a friend in the projects because she hadn't been down there in years. Lil Hak asked her to stay away from the projects.

A few months ago, her nephew took her out of the hood and moved Mrs. North into a mini mansion in an area called Upper Darby.

She looked behind her to see a young man running up to her.

"How can I help you?" She asked, seeing an awkward look on his face.

"Let me help you with the door. It's all about respect." Gee opened the driver side door for her.

"Thank you, that's so sweet. Who's your mother?"

"You worried about the wrong shit, little bitch."

"Huh?" Mrs. North thought she heard wrong until Gee pulled out a gun.

Boc…Boc…Boc…Boc…Boc…Boc…Boc…

Gee ran off through the back parking lot.

***

DOVER, DELAWARE

Lil Hak and Lez had been in Delaware, which was a few minutes out the city of Philly. They were trying to lock down Delaware with the drug game because it was a lot of money out there.

Lez had a lot of cousins out there trying to get money. He had been hitting them off with bricks.

When his brother Kilow was alive, he opened up shop out there for his side hustle and worked as a dirty cop in Philly.

"Facts bull, it's big money out here. We just got to clean up the city so we can control the whole drug track," Lez told him before Lil Hak's phone rang.

"Who dis?" Lil Hak answered his phone to hear a lot of dramatic shit going on.

Lez turned down the music because he knew those calls never sounded good whenever he received them.

"I'ma be back in a few, cuz. Thanks," Lil Hak said before hanging up his phone taking a deep breath.

"You good, skrap?"

"My auntie got smoked a few hours ago in Larchwood."

"Mrs. North?"

"Yeah, bro. I can't believe niggas violated like this bro." Lil Hak was good at hiding his emotional state when being around people. Right now, the death of his auntie was crushing him deep down.

"I'm sorry, cuz. You going to be alright."

"I know. Allah, got me bro," Lil Hak said, sinking into the luxury car seats. He was thinking back to when he was younger, and his aunt raised him and his other cousin.

***

ATLANTIC CITY, NJ

OG Kane and his wife, Vera came out to AC for a quick getaway and a night of fun. Going on dates and trips was something both of them valued because they had two very busy lives.

OG Kane and Vera sat at a card table, drinking Dom P and puffing on cigars. They were trying to win some money at the casino/hotel/resort that they always came out to.

"How much you lost already?" Vera asked, quitting because she'd already lost thirty thousand dollars. That was enough for her to call it quits.

"You mean how much I won?" Kane replied, smiling.

"Okay, papi. Bring home the bacon!" She cheered on her husband before telling him she was going upstairs to go to sleep.

An older gentleman, rocking a long beard, pulled up to the table and asked to join the poker game. Everybody agreed when they saw him dropping a hundred thousand in chips on the first hand.

Kane watched the gentleman and how smooth he was but there was something about him.

After an hour of playing, Kane started to lose and so did the man with the beard. He blew over five hundred thousand dollars with a smile. He got up and left without a trace or a name, but Kane saw he left a card. When he went to pick it up, it read, Kane leave Sosa Gang alone or you will end up like your Uncle Red.

Kane looked around nervously for the man who left the card but there were so many people in the casino. He couldn't see in or past the crowd.

Hearing his uncle's name sent chills through his body because before someone killed Kane uncle, he was being trained by him. Red's body was found floating in the river with body parts missing. Red was a South Philly legend. He had ties to the real Black Mafia. He was a hitman for hire and a drug connect.

Kane learned everything from his Uncle Red. The rest he picked up on the streets as a youth. His killing game came from just watching Uncle Red kill niggas daily like it was nothing.

Before his uncle's death, he wrote Kane a letter while in prison. He explained how he had made the worst mistake and crossed a close dangerous friend. Red never mentioned a name in the letter, but a few days after, Kane got the news about Red's vicious murder.

CHAPTER 27
DOWNTOWN PHILLY

Sosa and Zarhya walked through the Cherry Hill Mall, shopping for the last half of hour.

"Dior store," Zarhya said feeling like a weed smoker in a smoke shop.

"Damn, Dior?" Sosa stated, carrying his sister's bags and putting them down next to register. One of the store employee's watched their moves.

"Nigga, I know you not complaining," she said walking to the shoe rack.

"I forgot you're a shopaholic."

"Well, you shouldn't had invited to take me shopping. You know how I do," Zarhya told him before trying on shit that she planned to make him buy.

"It's sad that I got to make a trip to the mall with you just to spend time with my beautiful sister."

"I'm not trying to hear that cry me a river shit. You never call me no more and tell me I'm lying?" She looked him in his eyes, waiting on him to tell a bold face lie.

"You right, sis and I'm sorry. Real talk. I be going through mad shit," Sosa says seeing his phone vibrate. It was from his new lawyer, his dad's girl.

"Sosa, what the fuck do you really go through? You and daddy have the best life," she told him

"I just make this shit look good, sis. You have no clue what I go through every day out here in these streets. Don't downplay it if you not in it like me."

"Sorry, you're right. I be watching the news and reading the newspaper at school, praying I don't see your name," she testified, telling him the truth.

Every time she heard about a shooting in Philly, she automatically would assume it was her brother. Losing one brother, Block to the streets was hard enough for Zarhya to swallow.

"How's school?" Sosa changed the subject

"Good, about to graduate. I can't wait until this shit over. Oh my god, this studying shit be taking a lot out of me. Then, my boyfriend be driving me crazy." She paused not meaning to mention her boyfriend.

"Boyfriend?"

"Yes, I have a boyfriend. I'm grown now, Sosa. You just got to get used to it. One day, I'ma have kids and be married.

"Not right now."

"Boy, shut up. When it happens, it will but I love this skirt."

"What's his name?" Sosa wasn't leaving it alone.

"Damnnnnn ... Let a bitch breathe, bro. His name is Remeen. Do you want his birthday and ID number too?" She shook her head, knowing he was overprotective.

"I need to do my research."

"No, you don't. Worry about your new boo thang. I saw you post up on social media." Zarhya looked at him.

"Oh, you saw me?" He giggled

"Hell yeah, and she a baddy. Where you find her at?" Zarhya wasn't into girls sexually, but she had no problem acknowledging a bad chick.

"I can't tell you all that, but she may be a winner."

"I'm happy, bro. Karlee was a great woman and I'm sure you will always endure her love, but it's okay to open up and love again." Zarhya told her brother who was very tight with his love and opening up to other people.

"I feel you."

"I hope so."

"I'm going to see mommy in a few days," Sosa stated, seeing Zarhya stop trying on shit.

"Oh."

"You want to come?"

"Sean P Garrison," She called out his full name, something he hated.

"Stop playing with me in public."

"Well, stop playing with me. You know how I feel about her."
Zarhya had a strong dislike for her mom who ran off on them to
only become a psychopath.

"You have to learn how to forgive people. That's our mom, regardless how fucked up she did us."

"I know but I'm just not at that point in my life where I can up
and forgive her as if nothing never happened." She shot back ready
to get her items and bounce to the next store.

"One day."

"Maybe." She was picking up her new items for checkout as
Sosa saw Elina texting, telling him to stop by her office real quick.

Zarhya met him her, so she planned on going back to college
anyway. Elina's office was close so that was a good thing.

***

There was only one other person in the office when Sosa got to
Elina's job.

"Oh, right on time. Come to the back," she said, opening the
door all the way for him.

"Aight, how you been?"

"Great. Have a seat."

"What's going on?" He asked, seeing her grab some papers.

"The two men who recently got locked up for the shooting in
West Philly went to court today. Only one of them was able to get
bail because the other man is on parole," she told him.

Last week, Sosa asked her to go to court for two of Lez's soldiers, who got bagged for a shooting. Two people got hit but nobody
saw a thing.

"Okay. Get one out and still represent them for me. I will have
someone drop off a check for you in a few days. That's all?" Sosa
asked.

"Not just yet." She went to close her office door.

Sosa heard a change in her tone as she stood in front of him.
She sat on her desk with her legs wide open

"You straight?" Sosa tried his hardest not to get aroused as she
slowly took off her thong. She raised her skirt, showing the most
delicious, almond shaped pussy he ever saw.

"Fuck me. I want it so bad, Sosa." She bent over, giving him a view of her round shape.

Sosa was a man, and his dick was about to tackle its way out of his pants. He got his cock and slid his tool slowly into her opening.

"Ohhhhgggg ..." She moaned, feeling her tight pussy stretch to a ripping point. Sosa was moving slowly in and out.

Sosa picked up the speed and started fucking her with long strokes and deliberate thrusts.

"Oh, fuck, Sosa. I love this dick." She managed to get out as she lunged forward from the hard pounds he was giving her. He almost knocked the air from Elina's lungs.

Her pussy was clinging so tight around his thick tool. She thought she was in heaven. This had to be the most intense fuck she ever had.

She arched her back so he could go deeper. Every time he pulled out, she felt like her vagina was exiting her body also.

"Damn, your pussy tight," he said about to ejaculate.

"Let me catch it, baby." She pulled him out and tilted her head back as he splashed his semen all over her face. She also swallowed a mouthful. She continued to suck his cock so good that he almost buckled to his knees.

"Shit," Sosa said, hearing a knock at her door. He rushed to pull up his pants and she picked up her thong. She put them in her drawer. Sosa opened the door and a lady had a folder for Elina. Sosa rushed out, feeling guilty for fucking his dad's girl.

CHAPTER 28
DOWNTOWN PHILLY

Max felt like he hadn't been out in forever as he partied with a few of his boys in a nice, classy lounge. His boys wanted to go out clubbing but that wasn't Max's thing no more. Plus, he knew them Sosa Gang niggas be in them crazy clubs turning up.

Gee was supposed to come out clubbing with them, but instead, he chose to spend the night with his girl in their new spot.

Max knew it was a good idea to bring Gee into the Outlaws because he was a shooter and knew how to get a bag. When he heard about how Twin killed Gee's sister by accident when he was upstate, Max knew Gee would want some payback.

Sosa and his boys had been coming hard for the last two months. It had been non-stop shootouts on the Philly blocks day and night.

"Max." His boy Jif tapped him.

"Ayo, what's up?" Max poured himself a drink, watching the club go up on a Monday night.

"Somebody trying to steal your car in the parking lot," Jif said.

"What!" Max shouted, jumping up out his chair.

"Two dudes trying to steal your shit out back." Jif saw Max and three of his goons rush out. Jif stayed back and pulled out his cellphone to make a phone call. When he hung up, Jif took one last sip of Henny out the bottle and went out the other way. He got far away from the club as possible.

Once outside, Max made it to the parking lot to see nothing, but cars parked. He ain't see nobody.

Max felt something was off. He saw a gang of shooters popping up from everywhere, firing.

Bloc... Bloc... Bloc... Boc...Boc...Boc...Boc... Tat... Tat... Tat... Tat... Tat...

Max's goons were all caught off guard by Twin and his crew. Max took off running up the street when he saw his men hit the ground. Their bodies were getting filled with bullets.

Twin chased Max, letting off his Mack 11 compact submachine weapon, but Max was too fast. He ran like a wild man.

An all white Hellcat Redeye sped pass Twin, almost hitting him as he jumped out the way and on to the curb.

Max looked back to see a Hellcat on his heels, blow the horn for him to get inside. Seeing it was a female and not an opp, he stop running and climbed in the car as bullets were still flying behind him.

"You good?" Rika asked, drifting the car making a right and a left. She was speeding in the fast speed demon of a car.

"Who the fuck are you?"

"I'm da bitch that just saved your ass clown." Rika laughed.

"You got jokes?"

"Nah, but I'm Rika. I was in the club with you. I run with Foxy."

"You're an Outlaw."

"Facts."

"Thank you," Max said, seeing how cute she was when the streetlight hit her face and body.

"Sure, we fam. Where you going?"

"Let's go out to eat. I'ma get my car tomorrow, but you got a burner in here?"

"Yeah, two in the trunk for us." Rika always rode with heaters.

"Aight."

"What you want to eat?" She asked, driving down a strip full of restaurants.

"It don't matter. I'm sick about losing my men," Max said, thinking how Jif had to setup that whole little event back there because he was nowhere in sight.

"Shit happens."

"You right about that." Max couldn't stop thinking about Jif.

"Your name Max, right?"

"The only one in Philly."

"Is that right, bull?" Rika parked at a 24/7 restaurant next to a BP gas station. It was a diner with some good food. They enjoyed the rest of the night, talking and vibing.

***

ATLANTA, GA

Sosa arrived in Atlanta days ago, but he was having fun clubbing, shopping, and sightseeing with his new girl, Allure. Last week, the two of them made shit official and started a relationship. Sosa felt like he was ready to love again after Karlee's death. Even though, he knew her killing would never heal from within.

While Allure went out shopping again, he went to a mental hospital to pay his mom a visit. He hadn't seen her in a long time.

Walking into the crazy house, he asked one of the nurses for Ashley Garrison and she looked him up and down.

"Who are you to her?" The nurse asked.

"That's my mom."

"Are you sure? Mrs. Garrison?"

"Yes, my name is Sean Garrison. She is my mom. What's going on with her? Is she okay?" Sosa asked, seeing an odd look on her face.

"Take a walk with I'll bring you to her, but the visits are only for a few minutes," The nurse said while walking him through doors.

"Is everything okay with her?"

"No, she lost her memory, and she is suffering with a lot of illnesses."

"Since when? I mean I knew she had a few problems a while back," Sosa stated.

"She tried to kill herself twice and two staff members with a butter knife." The nurse brought him into a kitchen where he saw crazy people all over the place.

"Damn."

"There she is by the TV." The nurse pointed to the corner.

"I just need a few."

"Okay, she don't talk," the nurse told him watching him approach Mrs. Garrison.

Sosa saw his mom, who looked older, smiling at the TV. He stood in front of her, and she only continued to smile. Sosa shed a tear for her because he knew she was gone in the mind. He touched her hand, which was cold as his mom looked at him. Then, she looked at her hand. Sosa stood there for twenty minutes before leaving. He gave the nurse ten thousand dollars to look after her, but he was coming back.

CHAPTER 29
WEST PHILLY

Lez rode around by himself tonight, collecting funds from Lil Jet workers because he was with his pregnant girlfriend. Lez couldn't believe his little man had got a bitch knocked up because he looked at Lil Jet as a son.

Taking Lil Jet under his wing was a hard task because he was hardheaded and stubborn. As time passed, he saw Lil Jet soak up game and follow his lead.

He had to make a stop at 39th and Mount Vernon so he could pick up some money.

Earlier, Twin came by his crib and told him how he almost had Max outside of a downtown lounge. Twin said Lil Hak's cousin, Jif set up the whole shootout for a small fee but it went so sideways.

Lez had been trying to focus on money and handle his beef when the time came, but shit been quiet on the west side. The block was empty at 11:30pm because two cops were riding through all day. Jack shut shit down and sent everybody home.

Walking into the building, he called Jack and told him to open up the door. Seconds later, Jack opened up with a blunt hanging from his lips.

"Right on time." Jack let Lez inside the dirty apartment, which was a hangout for the gang. Three niggas was sleep on the couch with guns in their laps.

"The paper ready, cuz?" Lez asked, seeing Jack pick up a cup of Lean and start sipping.

"Yeah, I'm about to take a nap in this bitch. I'm twisted," says Jack, going to the back room where a chubby chick awaited him.

Lez saw a briefcase on the table open with stacks of blue faces lined up. Not trying to stick around, he grabbed the case and left the apartment. He made his way to his car. The windy night made Lez wish he wore his coat. He popped his trunk with a remote button and tossed the briefcase inside, closing it.

"You got forty-eight hours to get your crew off my block and I'm not playing," Foxy said, holding a Glock 19 to his face.

"Your block?"

"Well yeah, it's mine now. Facts. It's on you to leave or they can leave in body bags."

"Let me ask you something, because somebody gassed your big ass forehead up if you think I'ma let you get away with this. I will make your fucking life a living hell." Lez's words made her crack a smile and lower her gun as she stepped closer to him.

"My life is already hell." She was in his face.

"So you think, but you're burying a grave that you are not ready for."

"Lez, I'm always ready and wet." She grabbed his hard cock, making him jump. It brought a grin to her face.

"Get the fuck away from my car," he told her, mad that he let Foxy test him.

"Okay but forty-eight hours, Lez. I'll see you around handsome." She strutted off in a black Palm Angel hoodie outfit.

"Bitch." Lez knew he wasn't about to let her sucker him. He only had one choice, which was to prepare his goons. He had to make them strike on her crew and turf first. Tomorrow, he planned to send his hitters out.

Lez drove to one of his low key spots near Malcolm X Park. Every time he saw Foxy, old feelings popped up that prevented him from killing her. When they were a couple, they shared something powerful. He never loved no woman as he did her.

Parking in his parking spot, he shut off the car. He texted Lil Jet, telling him to be up and ready at 7AM so he could pick him up.

Climbing out, a car pulled in right behind him, blinding him with the headlights. He grabbed his pistol, thinking it was a move or Foxy. They flashed sirens before the driver door quickly opened. Lez rushed to tuck his gun under the seat.

"Why would you put your gun under the seat? That's the first place I'ma check, dumb ass," Janasi said in an exercise outfit, showing her fat cameltoe and flat abs. Her nipples were hard because it was a little cold outside.

"You followed me?" Lez asked, still sitting with one leg in his car and one out.

"I'm doing my job, Lez. You need to worry about that chick who put the gun to your head after you placed all that money or drugs in this trunk," she stated, tapping his trunk.

"You worried about me so much, how come you ain't help?"

"It's not my job to do all that extra shit. I'm DEA not Philly PD. Plus, I'm sure you can handle yourself. The two of you look like y'all had a connection."

"Looks can be deceiving." Lez got out of the car, seeing Janasia cross her arms and place a leg out.

"Listen, I know you don't want to go and do a life bid in prison. Lez, save yourself. I see so much good in you."

"You don't know me. Shit at times, I don't even know me."

"I can tell you're different. I watch everybody in your crew, and you stand out. I –"

"Save your bullshit speech for a rat nigga. Now, go to the gym in Fish Town as you do every night at 12 AM. Leave me alone," Lez went in his apartment.

CHAPTER 30
PICC MAX JAIL, PHILLY

Rizzy left from seeing his friend in jail at the PICC. He had been up there since 8AM so he was drained. He did whatever he could to hold his boys down. Visits, money on books, pics, drugs. Whatever they needed.

It was cold out so he was in a Calvin Klein sweater with a Peacoat while walking out of the gate.

Fucking with Kane, he never saw so much paper in his life. Money had been coming left and right. The only issue was beefing with two crews at once, but the Outlaws had been getting their soldiers up around the city. That was a good thing.

His relationship with Zarhya been going well. She was everything he looked for in a real woman. Growing up the way he did, love was a foreign word. When someone showed him real love and care, he fell deep within.

Entering his truck, Zarhya called on Facetime and he answered.

"Baby girl?"

"Hi, daddy," Zarhya replied, laughing leaving school.

"What you about to do?" She asked, seeing he was in his car.

"I just left the jail. I'm on my way to see you if I can get a second of your time."

"I'm sorry but I have to go to the DMV and renew my licenses. I fucking forgot about it."

"Okay. Go take care of that and I'ma catch you later, big head."

"Boy, bye hot breath." She hung up as he drove off.

Rizzy loved Zarhya's sense of humor. She joked all day to lighten the mood, but she would get serious at times. That would turn him on. Just the thought of Zarhya made him smile hard.

He made a left at the stop sign to hop on the expressway. Another truck creeped up on the side of him and opened fire.

Boc...Boc...Boc...Boc...Boc...Boc...Boc...

"Shit ..." Rizzy saw Wayne and gunfire as he hit the brakes. He saw Wayne drive off like nothing ever happened.

"Bitch ass nigga," Rizzy said to himself, breathing hard and thinking how much of a close call that was on his life. He knew Wayne from a photo OG Kane showed him of the D.C. crew and Sosa Gang.

***

Wayne turned up the YFN Lucci Wish Me Well 2 album in his truck on his way back to South Philly. Wayne had been at the jail since 8AM and that's when he saw Rizzy there visiting someone. He played the background all day even while visiting his childhood friend, Rakeem, who just blew a trial to get three life sentences plus fifty extra years.

The night Rakeem caught the triple homo, Wayne was there with him in the crib. Wayne was the one who pulled the trigger on all three men. Rakeem was the lookout. That night, someone who knew Rakeem, ratted on him after he told a female he did the shooting in South Philly that was all over the news.

Days after the shooting, the chick Rakeem was pillow talking to went to the police. Rakeem was arrested and what made the case stick was how Rakeem left hair and fingerprints at the crime scene. Unlike Wayne, who had on a ski mask, gloves, and sunglasses. Rakeem went in barefaced with his long dreads hanging, his worst mistake.

Wayne knew he missed Rizzy but he was sure he'd come back around so Wayne can finish the job.

***

WEST PHILLY
LATER THAT NIGHT

Lil Jet lead the crew on tonight's mission as he posted up in Overbrook, a hood ran by Foxy and her girls. Lil Jet saw over twenty chicks out hustling packs. He couldn't believe it because most of the chicks looked like strippers and Instagram models. They were so bad.

"How long we got?" Sling asked in the back, ready to turn up. He was clutching a Draco with one shot.

"Soon, Chew is parked at the end, Ap is in the middle, Lava is on the back end and we in the front but we waiting on Playa and Lion to cop." Lil Jet came up with a plan to have four cars full of goons blocking off the block. He had two old heads from his hood about to cop some work before he make his move.

When Lez told him about what he needed him to do, he couldn't wait to put on. Lil Jet was watching the block to see Beth car pull up. She got out to talk with one of the women. Lil Jet wondered what she was doing over there and how did she know the other women. Lil Jet saw Playa and Lion walk up the street about to cop some drugs and that was everybody's signal. Lil Jet got on his walkie talkie telling everybody to halt, meaning pause. Seconds later, he saw Beth get in her car and pull off. He was pissed because Playa and Lion already copped their work.

"Make a move, let's go." Lil Jet hopped out of the Toyota, first creeping with an AK-47 assault rifle with a 100 round drum.

Tat, Tat, Tat, Tat, Tat, Tat, Tat, Tat …

Sosa Gang niggas flooded each section of the block, shooting in the gun battle but that didn't last long against the high power assault rifles and submachine guns.

Rika shoots two of Lil Jet boys and Tahiry hits Sling twice before getting away with Rika. By the time Lil Jet and his crew left, there were fifteen people shot and seven got killed.

CHAPTER 31
SOUTH PHILLY

Twin just got done making his Isha (Night Prayer) in the Mosque with a few Muslim brothers, who lived a straight life and lived righteous. His father lead the prayer as always because he basically lived there when he wasn't home.

Imom Ahmad looked at his son while sitting on the carpet Indian style.

"Stay seated, son," Twin's dad Imom Ahmad said, seeing he was about to get up.

"As-salaam-alaikum, pop. What's up?"

"Walaikim-salaam, son. I want to tell you a story. There was a man named Freddy. He was a Greek and grew up into the ancient 18th century times. His parents were both servants for a king, who went by the name Troy. Freddy loved fishing and bringing back food to sell to the land people. That's how he made money. One day, King Troy brought Freddy to his castle and what Freddy saw next would change his life. Freddy's parents were both chained up in a cage crying and weeping. The king told Freddy that the only way he can save his parents if he fights three of the best fighters in his stable.

King Troy loved watching warriors fight. He would put on big shows in front of hundreds of people until one of the fighters died. Freddy agreed to the challenge and to everybody's surprise, Freddy won all three fights, killing all of the men. When Freddy asked the king for his parents, the king laughed in his face and told Freddy three more fights before he could take them. Freddy agreed and won the next three fights. Now, he was considered the best in Greece. Freddy went back to King Troy and before he could ask for his parents back, he saw his mom and dad beheaded already. Freddy was full of anger as the king laughed with his wife and servants surrounding him. Out of anger, Freddy grabbed his sword and attacked King Troy, killing him before people were able to snatch Freddy off of their king. As they were about to take Freddy to a torture chamber so they could kill him, the king's wife spoke. She told the men to leave him as she started to clap, confusing Freddy. The queen told Freddy it was all her idea to have his parents killed and kidnapped. She confirmed it was her who told the king to place him in the arena to fight for his life to see if he had heart. Then, she stated there was no doubt in her mind he would kill her husband for this vicious game but it was all for her sake. Freddy wanted to kill the queen but instead he married her and fell in love." Imom Ahmad got up from the rug.

"Hold on, what was the point of that story?"

"There are many points, brother but one is sometimes we want the wrong things in life. Even when we know how dangerous it can be, we still want it more." Imom Ahmad walked off, leaving his son with that.

Twin knew one thing. This wasn't those times. He was playing for keeps.

***

DOWNTOWN PHILLY

Sosa took Allure to his condo downtown because he wasn't ready to take her to his real crib. He knew she would question his income. At times, he would make little comments about his jewelry, luxury cars, clothes and his fancy expensive taste.

"I like this spot babe." Allure jumped in the bed with only a long shirt, fresh out the shower as he watched the news on the large flat screen hanging above the fireplace.

"It's cool."

"I wonder how you can afford all this shit. I know you say you're a businessman but what do you own? A billion dollar company?" She joked but wanted answers.

"I'ma be honest. I sell drugs. It's the only business I have Allure and I trust you to keep it a secret. If not, things can get bad," Sosa said as he muted the TV.

"Oh, well your secret is safe with me. Can we watch a movie?" She asked, nonchalant.

"So, you don't care that I sell drugs?"

"Sosa, I knew you sold drugs when you told me your name was Sosa," she said laughing.

"You had me under pressure this long," Sosa says, feeling all over her warm, smooth body and making his way down low.

"I know you not about to have me going crazy, soaking up these streets," she says as she felt his lips on her pretty pussy. He made love to it with his mouth.

He bit down softly around her clit and sucked on it like a baby bottle while he finger fucked her wetness.

"Ohhh, yesss," she moaned as he slid in another finger. It didn't take long for her to cum hard as juices flooded his face.

"You ready for this?" Sosa rubbed the tip of his tool in her small slit.

"Fuck me like you love me," she moaned, biting down on her lip and ready. He slid into her opening, stretching her. He was moving in slow, trying to catch a pace with her hips.

Sosa worked his entire length in her with back and forth strokes. He changed tempo in each thrust.

"I'm cumming again, baby!" She screamed, clutching the bed sheets as he started fucking her with more force. When he shot his load off, she laid him on his back and straddles on the dick She slowly let him sink in. Once he was in her, Allure bounced up and down, making her breast swing all over the place. The kitty kat was so good. Sosa almost passed out from dizziness. They did their thing for two hours, watched a porn movie and did it three more times.

CHAPTER 32
WEST PHILLY

Rika moved to a low-key apartment 49th and Lancaster when she started getting a little money thanks to Foxy. Foxy was pushing some many keys her way she felt like it was a movie she had been living.

Since her block recently got shot up, she had been laying low. Police been out there every day since the massive killing took place. The disrespect Sosa Gang placed on her made Rika's blood boil.

Minutes before the shooting took place, her sister came by to tell her she was falling back from the block and shit. When Rika asked why, the two got into a small argument on the block.

Beth ain't even give her a reason why and that pissed her off because Beth had been acting real crazy lately. That wasn't like her sister.

The doorbell rung and she stopped cooking her pasta to get the door. She was rocking booty shorts, showing her little butt with a tank top.

Most would consider Rika a tomboy unlike her sister, who was a girly girl.

"What the hell do you want?" Rika said, opening the door to see Beth.

"To talk."

"About what. You made it straight clear the other day."

"I was upset." Beth walked inside her sister's crib that she had been to many of times.

"A lot of shit been going down, and we needed you."

"I have my reasons." Beth took a seat, seeing Rika moved some things around to give the place a nice tasteful look and feel.

"Oh, so it's fuck me?"

"I ain't say that. You saying that." Beth took off her coat.

"We sisters, Beth. There is nothing in this world that will make me turn on you."

"Turn on you? That's how you feel?"

"Yes."

"How? Just because I don't want to kill or sell drugs no more!" Beth raised her voice, getting frustrated.

"I'm not saying that. I just want to know why."

"I feel like I don't have to tell you everything, Rika. You're not my mother or father. We sisters."

"Aight, you hungry?" Rika asked, not trying go back and forth.

"Nah, I recently ate. I came to see if you was okay. I heard what happened on the block.

"So, you came days later?"

"I saw you posting selfies on social media so I knew you was good."

"It was them Sosa Gang niggas."

"How you know?" Beth asked.

"Who else and I saw one of the little niggas before."

"Oh."

"This beef shit is getting crazy, and Foxy be nowhere to be found no more. Well, unless it's time to reup," Rika confessed, turning down the eye on the stove that her food was cooking on.

"Maybe you should fall back too. We both have enough money to open up a business and live a good life."

"Beth, I'm too deep in."

"How? That don't make sense to me at all."

"You wouldn't understand but I can't leave Foxy for dead. After all, she did for us. Unlike you, I can't turn my back on people at the drop of a dime."

"Rika, she left you to clean all her dirty work, Are you that fucking slow."

"This comes with the territory, and you know that."

"I have to go." Beth put back on her coat and left Rika's apartment without saying a word.

Rika sat there thinking on if she was tripping or not. Beth's stomach looked like it got a little bigger. Rika thought her sister was eating too good.

***

Downtown Philly

Barry had his driver take him to Elina's job because she left her phone at home this morning.

Being nosey, he scrolled through her text messages, and he came across a name that read Handsome. It wasn't the name that caught his attention but the phone number, which was his son Sosa's number.

Berry couldn't believe it as he started reading the texts. One read, *"Sosa I need to see you again please. That was the best I ever had in my life. Text me."*

Barry couldn't believe it as he read the next one that she sent him. *"I think I'm in love with your dick. I never felt this way Sosa and I know it's wrong but I can't help myself."*

Barry couldn't read no more. He couldn't believe his son and girlfriend crossed the line, but he planned to play it cool. Even though he was hurt.

Pulling up to Elina's job, he saw her pacing back and forth outside, looking nervous.

Elina rushed to his Maybach.

"You got my phone?" She asked.

"Yes, you left it at home. You got to be more careful love." Barry handed her the phone with a warm smile.

"I know, baby. Thank you. What you about to do?" Elina slipped the phone into her back pocket.

"Go play a few games of poker and enjoy the evening."

"Okay. I'ma call you when I get off work."

"Perfect."

"Love you."

"Love you more." He told her before telling the driver to pull off.

***

MIAMI, FL

Club Live was turned up tonight as Lil Hak and Twin both came out to the 305 to get away for a weekend. The city of Philly was on fire.

The police was running down on every block, arresting niggas for guns, drugs, old warrants. Whatever they could do to let niggas know the police run the city.

"I got to come out here more," Twin said, enjoying the scene as he played the bar with Lil Hak.

They was going to cop a VIP section, but it was already brought by some big name rappers in the building.

"All these bad ass hoes down here, bro. I need to get a condo out here." Lil Hak made eye contact with a sexy bartender, who had a fat ass with green eyes.

"I wish the gang could have came down here."

"Yeah, but Sosa super busy, Lil Jet laying low and little bruh got a baby on the way," Lil Hak stated.

"I know. How he beat us to the punch, cuz?"

"Facts. I don't even know who she got pregnant, my nigga."

"Shit, he don't even know who he got knocked up." Lil Hak joked

"The bull put that pain down with his youngins," Twin admitted.

Lil Jet had the biggest shooting that the city ever seen on one block since when the Black Mafia was running the city.

"Yeah, I respect his gunplay, but Lez told you how that DEA bitch been on his line, trying get him to fold." Lil Hak took a sip of his drink while staring at the bartender chick blush at him.

"Lez will never fold but I hope he don't do no dumb shit like kill the bitch. We got enough heat on us right now, bro," Twin stated.

"I agree but look, I'm about to hit this dancefloor with the bartender. You need to shake a leg, too."

"I don't dance, nigga," says Twin, seeing Lil Hak walk off as a cute brown chick approached him. She sparked a conversation that turned into a good vibe.

***

ACROSS TOWN, MIAMI

Max and Gee was out celebrating Max's sister, Prarie, who recently moved to Miami a few weeks ago. She working as a bartender. Prairie had her body done and was looking like a doll. Nobody could tell her shit now.

"Thanks for coming out. I love this club," Prairie told Max over the loud music in Club G5 as strippers performed all over the place.

"I needed a few days out of the city," Max told her, seeing Gee and his girl by the stage throwing money and having fun.

"You still in the streets, huh?" His sister wanted him to give the street life up so badly, but he was scared to.

"This is my life, sis. It's not that easy."

"All you have to do is invest your money in a club. Look at this shit, bro. These lame ass owners making a million every week in this bitch," Prarie told him, drinking some Ace of Spades out of a glass.

"I know. I'ma come up with something soon."

"You need to," she said as Gee and his girl entered the section.

"Yo, this shit is live, bro. I used to be in the cell thinking about coming out to Miami tossing bands," Gee stated.

"Oh, so you was dreaming about coming to trick on some dancer?" Gee's girlfriend Latifah said.

"Yeah," Gee replied, making everybody laugh, even Latifah.

Since coming home, the word fun was foreign because he been dealing with so much beef and stress with the Sosa Gang niggas.

He knew they would go harder on him because Gee used to be one of them. He knew they really wanted to make an example out of him.

Philly was hot all over right now. Him and Max thought it would be good to spend some time in Miami. At first, he was going to come alone until Latifah made it clear she wasn't going for that and she was coming.

Max's sister had been giving him the eye all night. She was his type, bad with a big ass, but Latifah was on his every move.

"I'm tired as hell," Max said ready to go back to the hotel.

"Me too. Let's slide, it 3:00AM," Gee stated as all four of them left. Gee played the back as Prarie slid close up on his dick, giving him a look. Luckily, Latifah was up front leading the way out. Gee had to control himself. Ten minutes later, they pulled into the Trump hotel parking lot in a rented Bentley truck. They all got out and walked into the lobby, where two other men was at. Gee thought there was something familiar about the two but he ain't want to stare and be rude.

Max made eye contact with Twin and shit went left from there. Twin pulled out his gun and fired shots at them.

Boc...Boc...Boc...Boc...Boc...Boc...Boc...Boc...Boc...

Two bullets tore through Prarie's upper chest, taking her down before Twin and Lil Hak slid out the hall away from the camera. They left two hoes upstairs. Max and Gee didn't have weapons because unlike Twin and Lil Hak, who drove to Miami, they flew out. Prarie died before the ambulance arrived.

CHAPTER 33
GERMANTOWN, PHILLY

Lez drove in a black Toyota Avalon with tints, following the BMW 540i speeding through the busy main streets. Lez was trying his best to keep up with the car without being noticed.

The person in the BMW was Kane. He'd been tailing him for close to twenty minutes now. Kane had a beautiful female in the passenger seat but Lez ain't care about that. Kane was going to get his issue today.

Every time he thought of Kane, he would think of his brother. Every time he thought about his dead brother, Kilow, OG Kane popped up in his mind.

Lez knew Kilow was a dirty cop with a lot of flaws out for his crew, but he never arrested none of his people. Kilow just tried to press them for money on some extortion shit and Lez knew this. He knew Kilow wouldn't get his crew put behind bars. He wasn't that fucked up.

Hearing OG Kane killed him from his old babysitter, sparked a rage in Lez and had Kane as his main focus.

The traps were all shut down until further notice because Philly PD was running down on Foxy crew. The whole city shut shit down until shit cool off because niggas wasn't trying to go to jail.

Lez saw the BMW stop in front of a hair salon and the woman got out with a Chanel bag, waving bye to Kane.

"Damn, she got a fatty," Lez stated out loud, seeing the woman's nice coca cola shape ass.

OG Kane drove off and Lez was still following him, thinking where was he about to go now as the BMW flew down the street.

He saw OG Kane enter a large parking lot connected to a big Mosque as people went in and out to pray and worship Allah.

"This nigga Muslim, damn," says Lez because he was a Muslim also. He be falling off a lot, lacking in his prayers and studying but he was still a Muslim.

When OG Kane walked into the Mosque, Lez's phone rang and it was a blocked number. At first, he wasn't going to answer but then quickly thought against it.

"Who dis calling blocked?"

"Wouldn't you like to know, Lez?" A female voice said on the other end and Lez knew who she was.

"What the fuck you want?"

"I ain't think you had the balls to pull a move like that Lez," says Foxy

"That's the warmup."

"Well, your warmup made shit hot, dummy. Maybe, next time you will think off wisdom and not emotion," Foxy told him.

"I'll make sure to keep that in mind before I blow your fucking head off."

"Somebody woke up on the wrong side of the bed, but I only called so you can hear somebody."

Foxy put someone on the phone so Lez could hear them muffled in the background.

"Lez, this is Dylan, your cousin. Help me!" Dylan screamed crying for help. Lez and Dylan use to be best friends before she went to college. Foxy knew this, so it was easy for her to trick Dylan into coming to her stash house.

"Foxy, your beef is with me, not her. I'll come."

"No, I want to save you for last but I'm sure you will miss your favorite cousin," Foxy said.

"Foxy when I catch –"

The phone call hung up on Lez as he was pissed off. Foxy was trying her hardest to make his life a living hell. He knew the only way to stop her was to take her out her misery.

OG Kane finally came out of the Mosque a few minutes later with his OG walk but Lez wasn't about to let him get away this time.

Lez pulled out his 50 Cal Desert Eagle and duck walked toward OG Kane.

Boom... Boom... Boom... Boom... Boom... Boom... Boom... Boom... Boom... Boom...

OG Kane saw Lez coming from the reflector of his car and fired first, trying to take Lez out. Lez was weaving and rolling all over the place.

"Come on, Lez, with your young ass. I'ma show you how a real OG do," Kane barked, looking for Lez.

Boc...Boc...Boc...Boc...Boc...

Lez popped up out of nowhere, hitting OG Kane in his chest but he had on a vest that saved his life.

Lez thought he had Kane until he bounced back, firing back at Lez as if he was never hit.

Boom... Boom... Boom... Boom... Boom...

Lez crawled under two cars as his clip slipped out.

"Damn it," say Lez, looking for the clip as Kane continued to aim and shoot at Lez.

With nowhere else to go and a lost clip, he went back to his car, ducking as bullets shattered car windows next to him.

When Lez made it back in the Toyota, he got the fuck from out of there. He was mad at himself for slipping.

***

WEST PHILLY

Lez pulled into the back on his boy Bryan's crib, who was a square nigga working a nine to five. He parked the car, leaving it there. He was about to call one of his young bulls to scoop him.

Walking out front, he paused when he saw Janasia leaning on a blue Kia and filing her nails.

"Firing a dangerous weapon outside of a public prayer temple. You and Mr. Kane. For some reason, Allah must not be on your side lately. People handling you as they say in New York. I was up there recently. People are sonning you," Janasia admitted.

"Fuck you. Do whatever you want. I don't give a fuck about nothing."

"That shooting your crew did is causing a lot of heat."

"Ask me do I give a fuck," Lez told her before walking up the street that had a few people outside.

"Your smarter than this, Lez."

"Who are you to tell me if I'm smart or not? You're just a dumb DEA agent trying to fuck over your own kind," Lez told her as he stopped.

"Whap …"

Janasia slapped Lez so hard she fucked up her own hand.

"You don't know shit. I could have been had your ass under the jail, all of you. I didn't because I'm trying help you!" She yelled now causing a scene.

"Don't ever slap me like that again and if you want to help, get on the team not against it," Lez said before walking off and leaving her standing there with her lips poked out.

***

SHARON HILL, PHILLY

Roddy's new girlfriend went and answered the door for Wayne to come in. Wayne thought Meghan was a cool girl for Roddy. She was cute, a nurse, had her own money and she took care of Roddy.

"Wayne, hi."

"Hey, Meghan, what you up to?" Wayne asked, walking in seeing her about to leave.

"I have to go to work. I'm a little late." Meghan's hair was wild, and her lipstick was all over the place.

"Don't let me hold you up."

"Okay, tell Abby I said hey." She ran out to her car with her coat because it was snowing out this morning.

Wayne walked inside the nice house to see Roddy at the table trying to roll a blunt while listening to Lil Baby.

"You been smoking heavy." Wayne scared the shit out of his brother, seeing him reach for his weapon.

"Nigga you ain't hear me ring the bell?"

"No."

"Turn the music down then." Wayne turned it down for him.

"I was getting a blow job by Meghan. That bitch head game so good I felt like I could walk again," Roddy said pushing his wheelchair towards Wayne, who was dying laughing.

"Nigga you crazy."

"I got that info you asked for. My boy Goody, who lives in York said Rizzy's family live on his block. He used to fuck with his sister but here's the address." Roddy handed Wayne a piece of paper before lighting his blunt of Cali weed he had sent in from the west coast.

"Right on time, bro."

"Kaba's mom had a stroke two days ago and died," Roddy said

"What? You serious? I just saw her at his funeral."

"I know, cuz. It be that stress though."

"Damn. Pay for the funeral and make sure his family good."

"Got you, but money's been slow since the police been hitting every hood," says Roddy.

"I know."

"When is shit going back to normal?"

"Sosa said next week. We just really waiting bro. Then, we finna flood this shit. I got some people in Allenwood I want you to reach out to and hit them off."

"Just let me know when you ready."

"Aight." Wayne left looking at Rizzy's family info, thinking about Rizzy and Kane. He had been losing sleep to the thought of killing them.

Since the drug flow was at a pause, Wayne was taking time out to make his enemy's lives not worth living.

***

SOUTH PHILLY

Lil Jet just climbed out the shower with Beth after a crazy steamy sex session in there.

"You really tried to put it in my butt," she said, hitting him in the back.

"I thought you wanted to try some new shit, babe." He laughed, walking into the bedroom in his low key apartment. He was there until shit died down a little from the crazy shooting he did in West Philly.

"I don't like anal, baby. It feels weird. I told you that." She saw a Snickers bar on the table and ate it before looking at her little tummy growing. She looked back at Lil Jet, who was more excited than she was.

"Come here. Let me dry you off," Lil Jet said seeing she was soaking wet just like him.

"No."

"Damn, okay. I forgot y'all women be having them crazy mood swings when y'all pregnant. I don't want no beef." Lil Jet threw his hands up, letting her know he wanted no beef.

"Kevin, we have to talk."

"Lil Jet heard her call him by his real name and knew it was something serious. She never called him by his real name.

"What's wrong?"

"Promise me you won't get mad at me," Beth said, sitting down on the edge of the King size bed.

"I'll never get mad at you, baby."

"You sure?"

"Yes, what's up? Let me guess. That's not my baby, is it?"

"What? No.. I mean, Yes, of course it's your baby, Kevin. I just have to come clean about something because I love you."

"Okay."

"The day I met you in front of the store was all a setup. I was sent out to set you up and kill you but the more I got close to you, I couldn't do it. I started making excuses as to why I couldn't kill you or why I didn't," she said seeing Lil Jet get up and walk around. He was shaking his head as she started to weep.

"Who sent you?" was all he could ask.

"The Outlaws."

"You're an Outlaw?"

"I was, but I told my sister I'm done with that life."

"Your sister?"

"Yes. We both worked for Foxy. She is our friend. When she put us on to this, we was all in for the money, but you changed my life."

"That chick you was talking to the day that block in the west got hit up is your sister?" He asked

"Yes, how did you know—" She paused before it hit her. He had to be the one who killed them people out there.

"How do I know you not staging this shit?"

"Kevin, I would never told you if I was like that. I really love you. I didn't even tell my sister that I was pregnant by you. I been keeping you a secret to protect you, baby because now you're a part of me."

"I can't believe that shit. I don't know what to think to be honest," he told her, seeing how disappointed she looked.

"I'm sorry. I just ain't know how to tell you."

"You found perfect timing."

"I'd do anything to prove my love and loyalty to you."

"Anything?"

"Yes, I swear."

"Okay. We will see but I'ma go for a drive."

"Be careful. They want you," she said, handing him his gun that he was about to forget.

York, PA

Wayne knew his way around York because back in the day, he used to get a little money out here on the Eastside on Eager St where he saw his first five hundred thousand.

There were a lot of Outlaw and Sosa Gang niggas in York. Wayne had no clue how big both crews were until he came home. The two cliques were spread out all over the state of Pennsylvania.

Driving on the westside, he got to a nice area called Dallas Town and looked for the house number 817, which was coming close because he drove past 810.

"Here we go," Wayne said, pulling over.

He watched the crib for ten minutes as it just started to get dark outside.

Wayne got out the car with his hoodie on and walked into the backyard, which had manicured cut grass and a small pool in the back.

Peeping his head in the kitchen window, he saw two pretty women cooking and talking. One woman looked like she was in her early twenties. The other woman had to be in her mid forties with a nice, toned body as if she worked out daily.

Thinking of a quick idea, he saw a small rock on the floor and threw it at the backdoor window.

Rizzy's mom and sister both looked, wondering what hit the door as they went to check.

When the backdoor opened, Wayne wasted no time and jumped out with his weapon aimed at their face.

"Go inside quietly. Who else in there with y'all?"

"My stepdad," The younger woman said, scared to death.

"Take me to him," Wayne says, following them inside as both women ass jiggled with every step. Their butts were so big.

Wayne saw a man sitting in the living room, watching the news and drinking a beer. When the man looked back, wondering why his wife and stepdaughter were behind him and not cooking his food, he saw why.

Boc… Boc… Boc…

Wayne fired four shots in the man's dome.

"Oh, my God, nooo …" Rizzy's mom cried.

"This your phone?" Wayne took Rizzy's little sister's phone and saw Rizzy's name in a few recent texts.

Wayne texted Rizzy. "Dis is Wayne, your friend. I knew I would touch your soul. See you very soon. No hard feelings.

"Are you going to let us live?" Rizzy's mom asked, hearing Wayne laugh before he blew her head off.

Rizzy's sister turn to run back but that didn't work.

Boc… Boc… Boc…

Wayne bullets hit her back, killing her and leaving her face down, ass up. He walked out the house through the front door with his hoodie low.

***

UPTOWN PHILLY

Zarhya laid on her back with her legs in the air as Rizzy muscled his cock inside of the tightest pussy he ever had. She was so wet that he felt like he was about to nut already, but this was round three.

"Yesss," she moaned as her sex muscles squeezed his rod with every thrust he pushed in and out of her.

Rizzy pounded away as she had an orgasm.

"Fuckkkk ... ugghhhh!" She screamed as he pushed her legs further back, hitting her dead end. He looked at the glimmer of her pink pussy lips as pussy juice trickled out her tiny slit.

Rizzy pulled out about to bend her over when he saw his phone go off. He looked to see it was a text from his sister. As he read it, his heart raced. Rizzy jumped out of bed and got dressed calling his sister and his mom.

"You okay, babe?" Zarhya said, sitting up and putting on her bra and panties, wondering if it was something she did.

Rizzy said nothing as he rushed out his crib to finally get in touch with his auntie. She told him his mom, sister, and stepdad were all killed in the house over an hour ago.

Rizzy rushed to York, PA, forgetting about the meeting he had tonight with the Outlaws.

Two hours later, he arrived at York Hospital and his worst fears were settling in. His whole family was dead. His brother was on his way up from Atlanta. Everything seemed to be at its worst right now but he knew who to blame, Wayne and Sosa Gang.

***

DOWNTOWN PHILLY

Allure woke up out of her sleep to see Sosa wasn't there, which made her put on his Gucci robe and see if he was there.

Tonight was amazing. They went to an Eagle football game and on a walk in a park before coming back to his condo to make love.

Sosa was the ideal man and that really scared her because she was head over heels for him. The other day, she found herself following Sosa around to see if he was cheating or even gay. He was too perfect. Something didn't seem right. Allure found nothing on him, and she felt bad for not giving him no type of trust.

Walking into the dining room, she found Sosa reading something.

"What you reading?"

"A Qu'ran. I just find some things interesting in it, but what's up?"

"Nothing." She kissed his lips

"You should be sleep. You got to take a flight to LA for your photoshoot."

"I know. Can you come with me please, papi?"

"Since when you use papi on me?" But I can't, ma. I got to take care of some things," he told her

"Okay, I guess. I'll have to play with this good pussy to the thought of you."

"I would love that," he said.

"You so dumb." Allure laughed as they talked for hours.

CHAPTER 34
NORTH PHILLY

OG Kane, Max, Rizzy, Gee, and Foxy were all sitting in the back of an old furniture store that Kane's people owned for over thirty-five years.

The room was silent, and everybody was sitting and waiting on Kane to start it off. Everybody had problems and so much grief they had been dealing with since going to war with the Sosa Gang.

"We meet again, and this is a blessing from Allah," Kane said.

"These niggas out here trying railroad us," Max stated.

"Facts." Rizzy thought about his family that just got killed.

"I salute all of you for standing strong in this storm and I must tell you, it will all weigh out," Kane stated as he saw his daughter laugh.

"How is that?" Foxy asked.

"You must think something funny," Kane asked, trying not to get upset.

"I'm just thinking. We're down on the scoreboard and you sitting here talking about some damn weather the storm. We need blood!" Foxy shouted.

"I agree," Gee added.

"Them niggas killed my family," says Rizzy, who had to bury his loved ones in a few days.

"I'm glad you all feel like this. I've found a location on Twin, and I want Foxy and Gee to handle it," OG Kane stated.

"My pleasure," Foxy said.

"I can't wait," Gee added, looking at Foxy, liking her work.

Perfect. Now that that's clear, how is the product moving now that we are back and running?" Kane asked.

"Everything moving good on my side," Max stated.

"I'm fine. Shit is looking great now. We opened up shop in Larchwood," says Gee.

"That's what I like to hear. How about you, Foxy?" Kane asked, realizing she had an attitude with him.

"My block still shut down," she told him.

"Why?" Kane shot back.

"Are you serious?" She gave him a dumbfounded look as if he asked a dumb question or something.

"No, I'm fucking joking. What do you think... I gave you a clear order to open up shop and that was all!" Kane shouted, raising his voice.

"Well, I ain't think that was too smart," she replied.

"Too bad. I call the shots," Kane told her rudely.

"Aight, I'll handle it," she says, rolling her eyes.

"I know you will, love." Kane smiled back.

"Everything is going to work out I think. We just need to start working more as a team instead of in sections," says Max.

"That makes sense," Rizzy suggested, thinking it was a good idea.

"So that's the idea. We work together. We Outlaws I'ma catch up in a few weeks. Let's show niggas who run the town," Kane stated.

Uptown Philly

Twin was at the steakhouse with his little cousin, who had just graduated high school today.

"I'm so proud of you," Twin said while he devoured some cooked steak on the grill.

"I know, but wait until I graduate from college," Wendy says, smiling bright.

"How's your mom? I ain't see her in a while now." Twin and his aunt didn't have the best relationship since he had been in the streets.

"You know she still mad at you for getting the house raided a while back."

"Gurl, she still on that?" Twin laughed.

"Facts."

"She'll get over it."

"I miss Triana. It was her birthday the other day and she was all I could think about, you feel me? We used to have so much fun." Wendy reminisced about the time she use to chill with her big cousin before she got killed in the slums.

"Every day I think about her."

"You still in the streets?" Wendy knew what type of life he was into.

"Why?"

"I just want to know because I see you in all this jewelry and you have a nice car out there.

"Wendy, don't ask a question you're not going to like the answer to," he told her seriously.

"Okay." She read between the lines quickly and left it at that.

"I have to meet somebody as soon as I drop you off at home."

"Cool, I have to check out some colleges in New York tomorrow anyway. I'm tired," she stated before getting up to leave.

"Damn, you doing it big. What college you feeling on the low?" He asked, paying the bill.

"To keep it a band, I want to go out to the west coast." Wendy walked out the restaurant, opening the door for him.

"Why the west?"

"It's always sunny." She joked.

"You chasing a boy."

"Hell no, I'm chasing my future," she told him at his car while seeing two people, a male and female creep up on them. Before she could say a word, it was on and popping.

Boc... Boc... Boc... Boc... Boc... Boc... Boc...

A bullet hit Twin in the head, taking him down. Foxy and Gee ran off into the lot.

Wendy panicked but she rushed to his aid and tossed Twin in the backseat of the BMW before driving him to the hospital.

When Twin arrived, to everybody's surprise, he was still alive and moving with a pulse.

The doctors were able to save Twin as his little cousin waited there crying and praying to Allah. It was something she never did but she was a Muslim woman.

***

SOUTHWEST PHILLY

"I can't believe this shit. We gotta go, skrap," Lil Hak told Lez who was chilling at his crib.

"What?" Lez jumped up.

"Twin got hit in the head, cuz. They just caught him lacking." Lil Hak grabbed two Glock 40 handguns and rushed out of his apartment.

"Fuck." Lez followed. Lil Hak recently coped a new Shelby Mustang to ride around in.

Lez climbed in the passenger seat and Lil Hak raced off, hitting eighty miles per hour down the small block.

"Who told you he got shot?"

"Sosa."

"He up there, and which hospital they at, bro?"

"Sosa up there now. I believe them niggas at Temple Hospital," Lil Hak says running red lights and almost hitting another car.

The person in the car he almost hit made eye contact with them while he blew the horn.

"Fuck you ..." Lez yelled, getting a little road rage but when he saw the driver of the Bentley, he almost hopped out the car.

"Ayo that's Kane." Lil Hak saw Kane to in the Bentley with a bad bitch.

"Fuck him, not right now. We going to catch him," Lez said as Lil Hak kept driving to the hospital. It took a few minutes to get to the hospital and when they did, Sosa, Twin's little cousin and his aunt was there.

"What happened?" Lez rushed up to Sosa who looked stressed and tired. He never saw his boy like this. Out of everybody, Twin and Sosa was the closest. He knew Sosa would take shit the worst.

"Twin went out with little cousin to the steakhouse, and when they were leaving got ambushed by a chick and a dude. She described the chick just like your ex girl," Sosa said, looking at Lez to his left.

"Most likely, it was her," Lez stated, knowing Foxy wanted get back from niggas hitting up her block and killing a gang of her workers.

"He finna make it?" Lil Hak asked

"The doctor says he is in stable condition. He in a coma I believe," Sosa said seeing Twin little cousin and auntie cry in the corner.

"Damn, cuz," Lez stated as Lil Jet and Beth, who stomach was poking out, rushed inside the hospital.

"Twin okay?" says Lil Jet as all three men look at Beth, trying to figure out where they know her from.

Lil Jet saw them staring at Beth like they were about to smoke her right there. Even Beth got nervous as she clutched her purse with her pistol in it.

"He's straight, cuz, but I remember her from Foxy block," Lez stated.

"I'll explain, cuz. It's not what you think, bro. This is my baby mother and she with me. That means she is with us," Lil Jet stated, seeing everybody look at each other as if a showdown was about to pop off in the hospital lobby.

"That's the woman you got pregnant?" Sosa asked calmly.

"Yes." Lil Jet shot back.

"Are you down with us or against us?" Sosa asked.

"I'm with him." She held Lil Jet hand to focus on who did this."

"Foxy and Gee did it," Beth said

"How you know?" Lez asked.

"My sister called me and told me they just shot someone in the head," Beth told them.

"Who is your sister?" Lil Hak asked her.

"Rika."

"We'll focus on that tomorrow. Let's just make sure Twin makes it out alright," Sosa told all of them before walking off to comfort Twin's family.

Lil Jet and Beth stayed there all night while everyone else went home to get some sleep.

***

HOURS LATER

Lil Jet and Beth had just got word from the doctors that Twin would pull through and be okay. He just needed a few days of rest. Beth was tired and hungry, ready to grab a bite to eat.

"You ready?" Lil Jet asked, coming from using the restroom.

"Yeah," Beth stated as Lil Jet helped her up.

"Come on, we out. I could see some Denny's and a nap."

"Boy, I don't want no damn Denny's. Do I look like a hood rat?" She shouted.

"A little." He joked.

"Don't play with me, nigga." She punched him in his back, walking out of the hospital.

"Girl, this can't be an abusive relationship."

"You want to get your ass kicked." She got in the luxury car.

Lil Jet hit the push to start, seeing Lez calling. He placed the call on the car speaker.

"What's up, cuz," Lez said.

"About to head home and get her some food," Lil Jet said, driving out the parking lot while the morning sun beamed on the car.

"You could have told us she was the one that you got knocked up, bro," Lez said not knowing he was on speaker.

"You do know I can hear you," Beth spoke up.

"Oh, that was no disrespect to you," Lez said before a car pulled up to the side of them.

"None taken ... Babe, look out ..." Beth shouted, seeing two chicks with guns out the window and one was Rika.

Boc...Boc...Boc...Boc...Boc...Boc...Boc...

Lil Jet raced off, making a right as bullets hit his driver side door but he made it out clean.

"You good?" He asked her.

"Yes, that was my sister and she saw me," Beth said.

"I guess it's no turning back now," Lez said on speaker before she hung up on him.

Romell Tukes

CHAPTER 35
TEMPLE HOSPITAL, PHILLY

Twin laid in the hospital bed, thinking about the close attempt on his life that happened days ago. He woke up from his coma hours ago. As soon as Twin's eyes opened up, the nurse told him he was shot in his head.

He remembered seeing Foxy and a male figure when his cousin shouted before being shot. Looking around the room, he saw posters of Scarface, which made him laugh hard as hell. Being in so much pain, he had to stop.

The room door opened, and he saw his father in a Muslim garment.

"This is the decreed of Allah, my son," Imam Ahmad stated

"Shit happens," was Twin's reply.

"Sometimes we put ourselves in these positions."

"True that."

"You just survived a head tap and now what is the key?" Imam Ahmad took a seat down in the chair next to Twin's bed, looking at all the IVs plugged into the wall.

"Only time will tell."

"Oh, is that right? I'ma let you know one thing about time. You can never get it back." Imam Ahmad pulled out a pocket size Noble Qu'ran and placed it on the highest shelf of the room.

"I know, pops."

"Good, I have to go but know next time there may not be a second time." Imam Ahmad walked out.

Twin laid there, thinking how he was going to grab the Noble Qu'ran from the highest peak of the room.

He knew everything his dad was saying but the only thing his mind was wrapped around was payback.

***

LOS ANGELES, CALIFORNIA

Allure was taking photos at an ice cream shop for a new up and coming magazine she was the cover girl for.

Things with Sosa had been amazing. He has been nothing but a true gentleman to her since day one. She was slowly falling in love with him.

She couldn't wait to introduce him to her mom and dad. She knew they would love him. Allure saw her phone ringing and saw it was Sosa. She went to pick it up, cutting the photoshoot for a second.

"Hey babe," she answered with excitement put him on Facetime.

"What's good, girl? What you up to?" Sosa asked, getting out of the shower and flexing his big arms and chest fresh from the gym.

"At my photoshoot."

"How is it?"

"Fun, I guess. I got a hour left out here. They pay by the hours. Then, I come back to you."

"I can't wait get back to you. Call me when you are done," he told her

"Okay, babe." She hung up, blushing harder than ever.

***

WEST PHILLY
WEEKS LATER

"These bitches think they can just do whatever the fuck they want. When have you ever seen a gang of chicks post up on the block to sell drugs?" Lil Jet asked as they were parked in a commercial van and dressed up as electrical workers.

Last night, Beth gave Lil Jet her sister's routine, and he couldn't believe it. She was really willing to give up her own blood for his love and that meant a lot to him.

"Niggas post up on the block all day and sell drugs. Why can't women if they want?" Lez asked, waiting in the driver seat. He was hoping Lil Jet's ways of thinking changed before he had a baby boy.

Two days ago, Beth found out she was having a boy and Lil Jet went crazy.

174

"Yeah, but in the middle east, this type of shit can't go down."

"Well, I got news. This ain't the middle east, cuz. Everybody got equal rights, men and women," Lez told him, seeing Rika come out from the back of an alleyway.

"That's a fact."

"There go our girl," Lez stated, watching Rika conversate with a group of women in a huddle for a few seconds.

"Twin is ready to get out the crib. He just texted me." Lil Jet read a text Twin just sent him.

Since getting out of the hospital, Twin had been at his crib relaxing and healing. He was trying to get right before going back in the field.

"He still don't know."

"About what?" Lil Jet played dumb as if he ain't know what Lez was talking about.

"Nigga, your baby mother."

"Nah, I'ma tell him after this so he can see how official she is, bull," Lil Jet stated.

"Aight. That nigga not going to take it as easy as me, Sosa, and Lil Hak because he just got a head tap."

"Yeah, by your ex bitch and you look like you still love her." Lil Jet joked but Lez ain't laugh one bit.

"She on the move." Lez saw a new red Infiniti Q60 coupe pull off, speeding down the Philly streets.

They followed Rika all the way to the Willow Grove Airport.

"What the hell is she doing? Beth ain't say shit about this," Lil Jet said seeing Rika drive into the crowded parking lot of the airport.

Lez saw two familiar undercover cops leaning on a Crown Vic with tints as if they was waiting on someone.

Rika pulled up in front of the cops and got out, looking around as if she was about to commit a crime.

"What is she doing?" Lez played the cut, watching the scene to figure out what Rika was into.

Lez and Lil Jet saw Rika hand the cops a bag, a camera, and a stack of paper while laughing and smiling as if her and the pigs were good friends for years.

"Wow, I wasn't expecting this, bro."

"This is odd but we about to find out soon," says Lez as Rika and the cops go separate ways.

They followed Rika back onto the highway as they ended up in Germantown at a nice condo building in a busy area.

"Damn, she lives out here?" Lez asked, parking down the street from where Rika parked.

"I ain't know it was out here, bro. Beth said South Philly."

"We can't listen to Beth no more."

"She did tell me every building Rika lived in. She had to live on the second floor and the first apartment on that floor." Lil Jet said.

"Damn."

"She's crazy, right?"

"Fuck yeah but put on your hat. She went inside. Grab a toolbox if anyone asks you know what to say?" Lez asked.

"We went over this a hundred times, bruh."

"Just making sure." Lez hopped out with the toolbox as if he was a real electrical worker.

***

Rika walked inside her real apartment, thinking about taking a nap. Tonight was a big night and she was nervous. Rika had a big secret that nobody knew about except the people she was working for, which was the ATF.

A few months ago, Rika agreed to work with the feds to bring down the Outlaws and Sosa Gang because the violence in Philly was out of hand. At first, the feds questioned her about two homicides. She quickly pointed her finger at Beth and Foxy to get herself out of a serious jam.

When the feds saw how easy it was for them to break Rika, they hired her to get deeper into Foxy's circle and squeeze as much shit she can out of Beth about the murders.

Rika had been busy taking pics and trying to get deeper into who Foxy's plug was, which was who the feds wanted mainly from the Outlaws and Sosa gang.

She got undressed about to take a shower, but as soon as she was walking in the bathroom, the bell rang.

The feds hooked her up with a low key condo, a car, jewelry with mics inside and money with GPS on it.

"Hold on." She put on her robe, knowing it had to be the feds with the wires for tonight to wear on Foxy.

When she went to open the door, two men kicked it in, pushing her to the floor. They dragged her by her wig across the carpet as she screamed.

Lez put his gun in her mouth as she saw who he was tossing his gat on the floor.

"Snatch me up some nice tools out the box, bull," Lez told Lil Jet as he popped open the toolbox.

"You niggas gone regret this shit."

"Fuck you … now I know you just came from the airport. Who was that?" Lez asked.

"Bitch, suck my pussy," Rika spat as Lil Jet couldn't help but laugh at her joke in such a crazy moment.

Lil Jet handed his boy a flathead screwdriver and stabbed Rika in the stomach with a clean shot, catching her by surprise.

"Ahhhhhhhhh fuck …" she cried in pain, holding her stomach as blood poured out.

"Now, who was you talking to?" Lez asked as Lil Jet rolled up a blunt while taking a seat.

"I ain't telling you hoe niggas shit," she said.

Lez went into the toolbox, pulling out a pair of scissors and clipping off both of her ear tips as she screamed. She was done and ended up giving in.

"I work for the feds. I was building a case on my sister Beth, Foxy, y'all gang and the Outlaws." she cried out.

"Bitch." Lil Jet jumped up and started pistol whipping her for telling on his soon to be baby mother.

'Let me clip off her toes and fingers," Lez said, grabbing a pair of pliers, cutting off her fingers as she barely moved. Lil Jet beat her so badly that her face busted open.

Lil Jet took the scissors and cut her tongue out before they shot her in the head nine times.

***

SOUTH PHILLY

Lil Jet went and picked up some clothes to change on his way home so Beth wouldn't see her sister's blood all over him. Even though, she knew the vibes.

The apartment was quiet. He hoped Beth ain't jump out with a knife or worse, a gun, trying to kill him.

"Baby," he shouted.

"Bathroom," Beth yelled.

Lil Jet walked to the bathroom to see her reading a Vogue magazine on the toilet.

"My nigga, you taking a shit in here?" He walked in on her, spraying air freshener.

"I'm pregnant so your son take shits when I do," she said.

"I never heard of that."

"Anyway, what happened?" She wanted to know since he left what was going to happen and was her info on point.

"Well, your directions was fucked up, Beth."

"What? You lying. Rika does the same shit everyday." Beth knew her sister.

"You was right about where she was at, but Rika made a detour."

"What kind of detour?"

"She had a meeting with the feds. She was trying to set you, Foxy, and us all up," Lil Jet told her.

"Damn, that's bad."

"Yep, she dead now." Lil Jet peeped something strange about her energy.

"Okay." was all she said

"You knew she was ratting?"

"Yeah."

"When was you going to tell me?" He asked

"After you killed her," she stated smiling

"You sneaky."

"No, I'm just being smart and playing the game." She flushed the toilet.

"I love you, girl."

"I know." She kissed his lips and went to grab some fruit.

Romell Tukes

CHAPTER 36
FISHTOWN, PHILLY

Kane and Foxy spent the whole day together for his birthday. It was his only request to her and Foxy agreed.

"Where you learn how to shoot like that?" Kane asked, taking a break from their paintball gun action.

They went out to a paintball gun factory to have a little fun and blow some stress off for Kane's birthday.

"I'm a natural shooter and I'm my own shooter," Foxy replied, realizing she broke a nail but she was cool with it. Spending time with her dad today was fun because they were vibing on other things besides business.

"How's your mom?" Kane asked, thinking about his ex-wife, who left him for dead in jail.

"She okay. I spoke to her this morning actually and she told me to tell you hey and a happy birthday."

"That's great. I'm glad she good but you need a personal life, Foxy. You have no kids, no husband. You're grown and blossoming. You're a beautiful woman. Live your life. That shit gonna be here for you," Kane told her, knowing she had no life because everything was business with her.

"I'm living my best life, Kane."

"You're lying to yourself."

"I don't trust niggas and I don't need the stress or dead weight." She used as an excuse.

"Tell me anything."

"I had this one love, but it didn't work out and to be real, I'm still healing," she stated sadly, referring to Lez.

"You have to move on. Don't block your happiness."

"Facts, but you have a beautiful wife. I can't believe I'm just meeting her." Foxy finally met her dad's wife, and she was bad.

"I guess this is the perfect time to you. I have more children," Kane said, looking at Foxy's unfazed look.

"Well, that's no surprise to me. When will you introduce me?"

"Whenever you're ready, I'll set it up but I'm happy you're understanding," Kane told her

"On another note, I can't believe Twin survived a headshot. That's crazy." Foxy couldn't believe when she heard Twin was alive. What was more shocking to her was the news of Rika's death. The gruesome news of Rika's death made every news channel. It was so brutal and vicious.

"Don't worry. You will catch up with them. Trust me, they too thirsty for blood," says Kane, knowing Sosa Gang was doing too much.

"I wonder who supplying them niggas."

"That's a good question."

"I got a friend, who is Wayne's girl. Tonight, I'ma go have a drink with her and hope to find out some info."

"That's smart because Wayne is my biggest threat," Kane stated.

"Why him?"

"Me and Wayne got history," Kane said, leaving it at that. Foxy found it odd that he didn't go in deeper on the subject, which made her think there was something else.

"Let's finish this game."

"Bet." Kane helped her off the floor so they could have some more fun.

They enjoyed the rest of the day together, having fun and spending time with each other as father and daughter.

***

DOWNTOWN PHILLY

Foxy and one of her close friends for over a decade entered a nice lounge in the downtown section of the city. Abby had been stuck in the crib with her man, Wayne for the past few months. They were working on their rocky relationship.

"You look cute tonight. Let me find out you trying leave with some dick. It's some handsome men in here tonight," says Abby, looking around. They made their way to the bar in the back of the lounge.

"Sometimes, I step out when it's called for." Foxy saw all the side looks from bitches and niggas as she sported a fire red satin Celine dress with red bottom heels.

"I see but I ain't heard from you in a few months. What you been up to?"

"Girl, I've been working on my website and clothing line," Foxy lied as the club DJ played an old Wale song she loved.

"That's good. I've been stressing a little, girl. Things are going downhill with my man so I needed this night out," says Abby before ordering a few shots to get the night started.

"What's going on? I forgot you even had a man, Abby. Facts, girl."

"I held this nigga down for years since a teenager. I gave my life to Wayne and now that he up, I don't even get respect from him. Sometimes he doesn't come home, and this nigga had the nerve to slap me two days ago because I caught him and a bitch texting. We got into an argument. I called him a fuck nigga and he slapped me." Abby shook her head, taking a shot and trying not to reflect on the night he violated her.

"He ain't have to do that." Foxy hated a nigga that hit on women because cowards do that. Foxy was thinking how blessed she was to be single and happy.

"Yeah, but the crazy shit is, I still love him, Foxy. I would do anything for him. It sounds dumb but you wouldn't understand."

"No, I won't. I'm not a punching bag so I can relate," Foxy said, taking a shot thinking how dumb Abby had to be. Foxy knew firsthand how love is blind because Lez took her through it before. Her and Lez had many arguments but one thing she liked about him was he never hit her or disrespected Foxy. He would always come back and apologize for getting loud.

"What happened to your boyfriend you used to be in love with?" Abby remembered a man who had Foxy on cloud nine.

"Girl, that was years ago." Foxy didn't want to talk about Lez, but Abby kept digging.

"Oh yeah, Lez. You talked about him all the time. How –" Abby cut her sentence short as she remembered Wayne telling Roddy a man named Lez's ex-girlfriend wanted him dead. Abby looked at Foxy, grabbed her purse and rushed to the exit in panic mode. Foxy saw this and followed her friend, knowing she put the connection together.

Outside, Abby ran to her car in heels, trying to dial Wayne's number. She knew the chick who wanted him dead. It was her best friend. By the time she climbed in the car, Foxy was right there on her ass.

Boc...Boc...Boc...Boc...Boc...Boc...Boc...Boc...

Abby's body was rattled with bullets as Wayne listened on Abby's line. Foxy saw a chick looking and fired two shots her way so she'd mind her business before disappearing.

CHAPTER 37
KING OF PRUSSIA MALL, PHILLY

Janasia had just got to the mall to do some shopping and pick up a few items for her cousin's birthday party. She was turning twenty-one and about to graduate college.

Today was Janasia's day off. She tried to leave work at home and in the office instead of carrying it into her daily life.

A few weeks ago, a woman named Abby was shot up in a club parking but weeks before that, a woman named Rika's body was found in an apartment. It was a gruesome scene.

Janasia found out the Rika woman was working with the ATF to bring down Sosa Gang and the Outlaws.

There was so much shit going on. She lost tabs on Lez, but she was recently on his social media page. He hadn't been active in a while, which Janasia found strange.

Walking through the mall, she had a lot of eyes on her because of her tight jeans that hugged her curves. The three-inch heels she rocked made Janasia look sexier. When she made a left next to a Lids hat store, her face dropped, almost bumping into Lez and Lil Jet.

At first, Lez had no clue that he was looking into Janasia's eyes because she looked very different today. Janasia had the nails done up, toes, skin glowing, hair curly, and he never could tell how curvy she was until now.

They was no doubt they both just caught a crazy vibe that words couldn't describe. Even Lil Jet knew there had to be something between them. Lil Jet spoke to Lez, who was having a stare down with Janasia, but Lil Jet couldn't deny his own sight because Janasia was a bad bitch.

"How you find me here?" Lez asked her.

"Don't gas yourself. I'm off today and I'm just doing some shopping and minding my business." Janasia gave him a fake smile while peeping Lil Jet look at her sexy manicured feet because he was a foot fetish nigga.

"You look nice though," Lez told her.

"I don't think it's smart to flirt with a DEA agent. When those words came out of Janasia's mouth, Lil Jet almost choked on his water.

"I'm not flirting. I call it honest," says Lez.

"Honest will be considered being honest with yourself first. It looks like the feds are digging around. A woman named Rika was found dead in her apartment and come to find out, she worked for them. So, I can only wonder who would kill Rika to cover their ass. Hold on, kill is an understatement. They overkilled her." Janasia saw Lil Jet's body shift as if he was uncomfortable with the conversation. That alerted her.

"Ms. Janasia, I have no clue what the fuck you're talking about." Lez gave her a truthful look but Janasia didn't buy it one bit.

"I guess there's levels to honesty," she replied.

"There's levels to everything." Lez shot a quick look at her perfect titties. He was really feeling her appearance today.

"We have to get going." Lil Jet gave Lez the crazy eye, letting him know he ain't want to be talking to no cop. He didn't want to talk to DEA, ATF, Fed or whoever, especially with a big Glock 27 tucked in his waistband.

"No need to be nervous, Lil Jet. It's cool. I'ma go but nice to see y'all. Somebody is moving real sloppy or it's all of you but when the feds get in the picture, it's hard to get them out. I'm DEA not FBI but y'all doing too much. Just to be honest as you say, Lez. Lil Jet, your gun is poking out. Take care, gentlemen." Janasia walked off.

***

"Who the fuck was that, bro? She know everything," Lil Jet said panicking.

"Relax."

"Nigga the bitch know my name and the shit with Rika. How the hell you know her, cuz? She was talking to you like –"

Like what nigga?" Lez cut Lil Jet off, seeing he was about to say anything out of his mouth.

"I'm just saying. The way she was looking at you is like she wanted to drink your dirty bath water." Lil Jet walked out of the mall and was on his way to set up for Beth's baby shower. They were having it today because Beth should be due in less than two months.

"You trust me?" Lez asked him.

"Yeah, why you ask that dumb shit for, skrap? Of course, I trust you. If I didn't, I wouldn't be here."

"Good. So, trust me when I say if she wanted us locked up, we would have been behind bars."

"I can believe that." Lil Jet added because he saw she knew about a lot of shit that would land them in jail for life.

"Janasia is odee smart. I been watching her, and she watches me. She a step ahead of Philly PD but now the feds in the picture. We need an insider."

"We don't know about that. That will turn into the feds." Lil Jet got a text from Beth, who was out shopping also.

"I'll figure it out."

"That DEA chick like you, I can tell, and she bad."

"She don't like me, bro. All she want is a nigga to snitch. They all play that game."

"Whatever you say." Lil Jet laughed, getting into his car and placing the bags in the back.

Romell Tukes

CHAPTER 38
SHARON HILLS, PHILLY

Roddy may have been in a wheelchair for life but that didn't stop him from sipping Lean day and night. His girl, Meghan tried to beg him to stop but he refused. So, two days ago, she left.

Wayne had been so depressed since Abby got killed. He turned to the Lean too, now. That bothered Roddy because Wayne was never the druggy type and he felt responsible.

The doorbell rang and Roddy was waiting on some shit that he ordered online from Amazon a few weeks ago.

He wheeled himself but he was half-drunk from the Lean he had been sipping since he woke up this morning. Getting closer to the door, something told him to pick up his Draco from the living room floor. Shit been getting crazy, and he didn't want to be another victim.

Opening the door, Roddy almost shitted on himself when he saw Kane standing there with a dozen of red roses.

Roddy slammed the door on Kane's foot and raced off in the wheelchair, trying to get into the living room where his weapon was laid out and awaiting him.

When Roddy made it to the doorway of the spacious living room, Kane flipped his chair over and kicked him twice.

"Ahhh…" Roddy groaned in pain, trying to crawl until Kane grabbed his swollen ankles.

"Relax, young bull. I just want to talk." Kane placed his pistol in Roddy's face while taking off his coat.

"You take advantage of the cripple, bitch ass nigga." Roddy spat, leaning on the wall and hoping Kane didn't try no crazy shit.

"I used to see you and Wayne run around the streets before I went to prison and deep down, I knew you two would be special. While in jail, I took Wayne under my wing and gave him the game like he was my own son," Kane stated, telling a story and kneeling down.

"Nigga you ratted on Wayne"

"I won't call it ratting. I'll say he helped me gain my freedom back. Now, that's loyalty but when you sitting in jail with a life sentence, your mind starts thinking different. The walls start talking to you," Kane says with a crazy look in his eyes.

OG Kane had a rough bid. In and out of the box, stabbing inmates and correctional officers.

Being locked up so long, he started thinking of ways to get out of prison and Wayne was one of his plans. Wayne was selling work for him and supplying the city with drugs Kane was getting still while in jail because his plug loved Kane.

The day Wayne caught his murders, nobody knew Kane paid the niggas to get at Wayne, knowing he would put in some work. Kane became a mastermind in his cell, especially reading books from Robert Green and even hood novels by Romell Tukes, kept his mind sharp on the street shit.

"That's not law or real, my nigga. You a bitch made nigga, using good men to live out your dreams because deep down you're a straight –"

Boc… Boc… Boc… Boc… Boc… Boc… Boc…

Kane looked at Roddy take his last breath on the floor.

OG Kane was finna tell Roddy a little story of how he used to fuck his mom, but he couldn't continue to be disrespected by being called a bitch. He planned to get Wayne ASAP because Kane didn't want his secret of him being a rat to get out in the street. He had to protect his pride. OG Kane saw well known rats in the streets chilling every day. The new era was different from back in the day.

Dudes was ratting now and coming home litty. Kane been thinking lately about forming a crew of all gangsta rats and shutting shit down.

***

TEMPLE HOSPITAL, PHILLY
ONE MONTH LATER

Beth had an early delivery this morning and the baby boy arrived at 1pm. His son, they named Kevin Jr., came out six pounds and handsome. He looked just like his mommy and daddy.

Lil Jet had been holding his son all day, playing with the little toddler in his arms and admiring the baby he created.

"I got to have me a little one soon," Lez stated.

"Me too," Lil Hak said in the corner.

"Man, none of you niggas need no kids. Y'all going to have them little fools out here blowing shit up at ten years old," Sosa stated with his girl Allure there with him. Today, he introduced her to the gang, and they thought she was valid and his type.

"You ready to be a father?" Twin asked, speaking for the first time today. He wasn't feeling Beth being his young bull's baby mother, but he had no choice but to respect it.

"Yeah, I feel like a real man today. I'm focused on fatherhood so don't call me for a few months and I'm changing my number," Lil Jet joked, making everybody laugh.

"Boy please, you might not stay in the house five minutes," Beth said, holding her child.

"That's a fact." Lez added.

The crew chilled with Lil Jet and Beth for another hour before everybody left. Lil Jet had just bought Beth a little house in Darby and when she left the hospital, she was shocked to see the house set up. It was ready with a baby room and all it brought tears to Beth's eyes.

CHAPTER 39
WEST PHILLY

Lez drove to his crib on a late night. He was coming from a club with Lil Hak and a few soldiers. He had been drinking all night, but he was not fucked up, just tipsy.

With two apartments, the one in West Philly is where he planned to spend the night because it was closest to the club that he just left.

Lil Jet wanted to come out, but he was at home parenting with Beth. He had really been seeing Lil Jet's growth in the recent days as they shared conversations about opening businesses in the black urban areas.

He parked the gray Range Rover outside of the building and looked around, on alert for his safety. Getting caught slipping wasn't about to be his history.

The winter weather was starting to break, and spring could be felt. Lez knew this coming summer was going to be the coldest the city ever saw.

Walking into his building, he saw a missed call from Wayne. He called him back, already knowing he needed someone to talk with.

Losing Roddy fucked Wayne up and Lez understood the grief. Just the thought of losing someone would really fuck up anybody's mental.

"What's good, bull?" Lez answered

"Ain't shit, cuz. I heard y'all was in the club turned up tonight. I'm in my bag though because nobody invited me," says Wayne.

"That was some spur of the moment type shit, bro."

"I bet but Roddy's funeral going to be this weekend. I'm just letting the guys know, cuz," Wayne told him.

"We all there. Believe that and stay strong. It's going to be our time soon." Lez walked into the crib, closing the door and ready to take a nap.

"That's the plan but I'm straight, skrap. I know that this shit comes with the game," Wayne replied.

"I'ma go to sleep. Hit me in the morning."

"Facts."

When Lez hung up, a cold steel object was pressed against his dome.

"Try some slick shit," a female voice says from behind him.

"Do what the fuck you do."

"I don't know why Foxy ain't been let me kill you."

"Bitch, you boring the shit out of me. Let's get this shit over with, sweetheart," Lez said as she turned him around. He saw a young, cute chick that he didn't recognize but Lez could tell she was young and full of anger.

"Why is it that Foxy wants to always spare you?" Tahiry asked.

"Go ask her."

"I don't like your mouth or you period." She traced the gun around his forehead.

"Listen, whoever you are, my time is valuable. So, either kill me or get the fuck out. I will hunt your young ass down and kill everything you ever loved."

"I'm starting to see why Foxy is in love with you," Tahiry said, tracing her gun down his penis.

"If you wanted to suck my dick, all you had to do was ask."

"Maybe, I do but I prefer to blow your head off. I hate all of you Sosa Gang niggas" she said, licking his ear and backing up.

"Save me the memory. You're fucking burnt out," Lez stated as she wrapped her small finger around the trigger.

"Bye, Lez."

Boc… Boc… Boc… Boc…

Lez saw blood burst out of Tahiry's chest before her body slumped over him. Lez looked toward the door and saw Janasia standing there. She was aiming her weapon and looking at him to make sure he was good.

"You good?" She asked

"Yeah." He looked at Tahiry's dead body on the floor.

"You have to go so I can call this in."

"Thank you."

"Sure." Janasia called it in, reporting the shooting as if Tahiry aimed and was about to fire at her.

Lez left before a gang of police arrived in his apartment to investigate the killing. Janasia told them she saw Tahiry break into this apartment to steal and when she entered, Tahiry aimed her weapon at her.

***

YORK, PA

OG Kane took a trip out to pay someone a visit because he found out some news that really bothered him.

Two months ago, he hired a private investigator to see what his wife, Vera had been doing in York because she was spending a lot of time there.

He knew she did mostly all of her real estate business in York, but he felt like there was a little more to it than what she was showing. Hiring the P.I. to watch her came in handy for Kane because he found out Vera had a son in York, who played basketball at the high school.

Hearing that news crushed his heart to the point he couldn't even look at Vera for a few days now. The private investigator told her everything he needed to know about the kid, Prince, who was a teenager.

OG Kane knew Prince wasn't his because he been in prison for the last two decades. Vera had to have a seed with someone else and she never mentioned it.

School was out and Kane cruised through the school parking lot looking for Prince.

In a crowd of kids, Kane saw Prince laughing with a basketball in his hand.

***

"Man, y'all crazy," Prince told his basketball team, who was all leaving school and getting ready for their game tonight in Allentown.

"Y'all going to that party on Friday at Karena's house?" Prince's best friend Malcolm asked everybody. The whole crew agreed, down for a party. Plus, it gave them something to do Friday night instead hang around town.

"I can't wait. I'ma fuck Karena this weekend," Prince stated.

"She don't want your black ass. You know she boujee," another kid stated.

"Don't hate," Prince said.

"Can I get a ride?" Malcolm asked Prince.

"Yeah, let's get away from these busters," Prince said, breaking off with the basketball team.

"You think Karena really going to give up the pussy?" Malcolm asked, walking to Prince's new Honda Civic Type R that his mom got for him two weeks ago. Prince was a mama's boy, even though his auntie took care of him.

Pulling up at his car, an older man parked behind his Honda and hopped out. By the time Prince and Malcolm saw the gun, it was too late.

Psst... Psst... Psst... Psst... Psst... Psst...

OG Kane jumped back in his car and drove back to Philly after killing Prince and Malcolm with a 40 Glock with a silencer attached to it.

***

OG Kane walked into his house, hours later, to see Vera crying in the living room.

"You good baby?" Kane asked, seeing something wasn't right but he already knew.

"I just lost a family member. My sister called a few seconds ago." She was crying and trying to not break all the way down.

"I'm sorry to hear that, Vera."

"I have to go. I'ma be back later." She jumped up and left.

OG Kane called for her as if he was worried but deep down, he couldn't stop laughing. Kane told her years ago loyalty was equal to death in his book.

CHAPTER 40
UPTOWN PHILLY

Wayne and his gang were all at Roddy's funeral paying their respect to a fallen soldier that the crew loved. Roddy's death hit the D.C. crew hard. They were ready to turn up a notch more than what they were doing now.

The funeral was so packed in the church. Police had come out to direct traffic and to make sure nothing went down because half of Philly's gutter came out.

Sosa sat next to Wayne as the rest of the gang played the background and yearned for revenge.

"You straight dog?" asked Sosa, seeing Wayne head low, as family members went to the stage to speak good about Roddy.

"I'm good," Wayne says, seeing two youngins in long trench coats, acting strange. Even Sosa saw their funny movements but he tried to still be at ease.

When everybody saw the two women walk up to the stage, making their way by the pastor, whispers called be heard. Some said those were Roddy's mistresses or his whores.

"I'm glad everybody came out today for Roddy. He was loved from a wheelchair," the woman said with an evil smirk as everybody in the crowd looked at each other.

"Who the fuck is that?" Wayne stated.

"I ain't really know Roddy bitch ass but if he was alive, I would have loved to kill him. That's the life of an Outlaw and Foxy sends her regards." The woman pulled out a Draco from under her trench coat and the other women next to her did the same.

Tat... Tat... Tat... Tat... Tat... Tat... Tat... Tat...

Wayne and Sosa hit the floor as others ran for cover. The pastor was an off-duty cop, who tackled both women and with the help of other church civilians, placed the women in ties as if it was cuffs.

Two people got fatally shot. One person was an elderly woman, who had been a part of the church for over twenty-nine years. The other person, hit in the neck, was a new Sosa Gang member who came with Lil Hak. He got caught in the crossfire.

Wayne and Sosa couldn't believe Foxy had the balls to pull some crazy shit like this inside of a church. Outside, police and ambulance were all over the place. Wayne and Sosa's crew got the fuck out of there.

Wayne asked his people not to bring no guns in the church but now he regretted it.

"I know something was wrong with them bitches!" Wayne shouted to Sosa in the backseat of a Bentley truck.

"They going to pay." Sosa meant every word.

**

GERMANTOWN, PHILLY
DAYS LATER

Barry saw Sosa walk into Chart House restaurant in a suit, looking like a real businessman.

"Look at my boy. You remind me of the old me back in the day," says Barry, hugging his son

"Stop with the fake shit."

"How you been?"

"Out here trying to stay alive and make big money moves."

"Shit, you been copping so much product that I had to double up on my orders. Your little crew are the hardest pushers I've seen in a long time." Barry told him, taking a sip of wine.

"We doing what is supposed to be done out here, but it's also about giving back. I heard the city YMCA is about to be shut down, due to lack of a finances, so I'ma buy it."

"That will keep the Philly PD off your ass."

"How you know they on my ass?" Sosa asked.

"I know everything," Barry repeated, giving him a deep look hoping he could read between the stare.

"Well, we having a big issue with a dude name Kane, his daughter and now his crew."

"I thought he got out of prison on ratting or some shit?" Barry asked.

"Man, I don't even know. All I know is he got these fools out here trying take out heads off."

"I hate that bitch nigga, but on another note, how's your mom?"

"I'ma go see her soon. I don't want her in Atlanta alone. She lost it."

"I think you should let sleeping dogs lay. Your mom has demons you know nothing about," Barry told him.

"Don't we all, but I got to go. Call me when it's time. I got everything in order." Sosa stood up and left not catching his dad's scroll face.

***

TEMPLE UNIVERSITY, PHILLY

Zarhya was cleaning up her dorm room for Rizzy to stop by so she could get some good dick. She was fresh off her period and needed some good loving. College was going great. Her grades were good. The least was a B+.

"Coming." Zarhya turned down the stereo, hearing the knock at the door.

Rizzy walked in and she jumped in his arms if she haven't saw him in years.

"Babe." She kissed all over his face.

"What's up?" Rizzy seemed a little off and she peeped he wasn't himself.

"Just cleaning. Sit down and let's watch a movie. How about Bad Boy 3?" She suggested turning with her booty shorts stuck in her phat ass.

"I don't think that's going to happen." Rizzy's voice got cold as he pulled out a 9mm handgun and attacked her.

"Nooooooo!" She screamed as Rizzy started pistol whipping her until he thought she was dead. Blood was everywhere and chunks of her flesh were all over the place.

"Bitch," Rizzy said, leaving and shutting off her room light.

A few days ago, Rizzy got the scoop on how Sosa had a sister in college named Zarhya. Foxy had chilled with her and Sosa a few times. Rizzy didn't shoot her because he ain't want to alert other students, so he planned to pistol whip her to death.

Rizzy had no heart life after his family was murdered. He wanted anybody who had any connection to Sosa Gang.

***

Erica was walking through the college campus on her way to Zarhya's crib to see her friend.

Erica wanted to go out tonight and have a drink with Zarhya if she wasn't busy.

On the way to Zarhya's dorm, she walked past a handsome man wearing white but as she got closer in the light, there was a big blood stain on his shirt.

The man must've not seen the blood because when he looked at what she was staring at, he tried to cover it.

Erica walked past him, getting a weird vibe from him as she walked into the dorm building, listening to Tyga on her iPod.

Once at Zarhya's room, she knocked over twenty times before realizing the door was open. When she walked inside, Erica saw blood stains and when she took a few steps deeper into the room, her body froze.

"Ahhhhhhhhhhhh …" She ran out the room yelling, screaming and calling for help.

Erica was scared to even touch Zarhya. She ran next door while calling 911 for her best friend.

CHAPTER 41
DOWNTOWN PHILLY

Sosa just had six of his boys get arrested and the only person who could get them out was Elina. He came out to pay her a visit today.

"Is Elina in?" Sosa asked the secretary, who gave him a nasty look.

"One minute, she's with a client. You can just have a seat," the white lady stated.

"Rude bitch," Sosa mumbled under his breath before sitting down.

Sosa felt weird coming back here because the last time he was in Elina's office, he ended up fucking the shit out of her. Sosa couldn't even lie if he wanted to. Elina's pussy was great. She had some wetty.

Elina and her client walked out with all smiles.

"Thank you so much. Have a good day," Elina told her client before she saw Sosa sitting in the lobby.

"Sosa, come in. How can I help you?" says Elina, acting professional in front of her secretary.

"I need your help," Sosa said, walking into Elina's office.

"I bet he do," the white lady mumbled as she watched their moves until the office door closed.

"What's wrong, Sosa?"

"Six of my people got booked. Half on murder charges and the rest on drugs," Sosa told her.

"Do you have their names?"

"Yes." He dug into his pants and pulled out a piece of paper with names on it.

"I'll get right on this, but it's going to be a little hard to get a bail on the murders right now. I'll see if I can use my juice." She smiled, trying not to think of what happened last time on her desk.

"Thanks, but how's everything?"

"Good, but I been waiting to see you, Sosa. I texted you a lot and no reply."

"That's because you're my dad's piece and it don't feel right," he told her.

"I get it, but I want you to know something. Barry is not to be trusted, Sosa. He really don't like you. He's only using you. I heard him bragging to someone how you will end up like Block real soon."

"Elina, you can't feed my brain with whatever you're trying to do, so I'ma leave. Call me when that's done." Sosa didn't want to hear no more as he got far away from her office.

***

YORK, PA
WEEKS LATER

Vera had to bury her son two weeks ago and she still felt the pain. Prince's death was still unsolved, and Vera found that very odd. She had been digging into her son murder by herself and today she may have gotten a break.

One of Prince's ex-girlfriends got in touch with Vera on Facebook, asking to meet up with her at a small deli near the high school. Vera awaited in the deli for the young woman, seeing her daughter Allure text her phone.

Vera still held the secret back from Kane about her son, but Allure knew the real truth.

A young girl walked into the deli wearing sunglasses, and a sundress. Vera saw her a few times with Prince last year until he found a new girl.

"Vera."

"Yes, how are you doing? Have a seat."

"Thanks for coming, I'm Ashley. Me and Prince had something special until he started dealing with a cheerleader. The day he got killed, I was waiting to speak to him about prom because I still wanted him to take me as he promised. I waited in the parking lot so I can talk to him one on one. When he got around other people, especially his basketball team, he would act differently. I waited near his car in the cut. When I saw him coming to his car, I saw a gray Maybach creeping on him. At first, I thought it was a nice car.

Then, I saw the brown skinned man with the scar on his face, lean out the window with a gun and kill Prince and his best friend." Ashley's eyes got watery as she had to live with it.

"The Maybach had anything on it that stood out?" Vera asked, putting shit together because she had a feeling the young girl was telling the truth. Three more kids said they saw a gray luxury car leave the lot.

"Uhhhhhhh, yes. I just remembered I saw a yellow sticker that read Allah on the trunk."

Vera felt her heart drop in her lap. Vera knew that car belonged to Kane because she is the one who gave him the yellow sticker that read Allah for his car.

"I thank you Ashley, but have you told anybody else about this?"

"No not at all. I was scared. You're the only person I told."

"Make me the last. Keep this between us, okay," Vera said before leaving in a rush.

"I will promise," Ashley said crying and mad that someone took her first love, who had a bright future.

***

DARBY, PHILLY

Lil Jet finally got the hang of feeding his son with the baby bottle. Being up all night and waking up at different hours of the night was something he'd been trying to get used to.

His son didn't cry too much unless he was hungry or had to take a shit. Then, Lil Jet would change his diaper.

Lil Jet never knew taking care of a baby could be harder than it looked but he loved it. Seeing a little him softened his heart. He was starting to feel soft at times.

Beth laid in the room, sleep from the long night they had being parents. Lez had been calling all day but Lez told him he would get at him when Beth got up. Lil Jet was glad the gang all accepted Beth because she began a part of him. Now, they were family. Beth was screaming out Sosa Gang now and he always got a good laugh out of her.

CHAPTER 42
DOWNTOWN PHILLY

Sosa rushed to his condo so he could take a quick shower before he picked up Allure from the airport. Two days ago, four of his goons on Lil Hak's side were released on bail. He hadn't had a chance to thank Elina yet.

He parked his Bentley SUV next to his Audi in the lower garage area of the build.

One foot out of the car, he heard his name being called, which made him pull out his gun on defensive.

"It's Elina. Put the gun down, please. We need to talk."

"Elina, what are you doing here?"

"Sosa, we have to talk. There is a lot of shit going on," she said.

Sosa looked at her coat, thinking he had to be tripping or some shit. He looked at the three big yellow letters on her jacket that read FBI.

"What he fuck are you talking about?" he stepped back looking around.

"Nobody is here but us, Sosa. I'm not only a part time lawyer but I'm a FBI agent, who been investigating your father for seven years," she admitted.

"My nigga, you can't be serious, I just fucked you." He raised his voice.

"I know, Sosa. That was a mistake but please lower your voice. Your father is going to kill you. He's been using you and your crew to kill all his opps. We have him on lots of wiretaps on plotting your murder. You have no clue how really dangerous your father and mother is."

"My mother?"

"Yes, she escaped from the mental hospital. We had a close eye on her. Do you remember that nurse woman you paid to look after your mom?"

"Yeah." Sosa couldn't believe his ears.

"She was one of ours, but your mother is why your dad is who he is, Sosa. Soon, everything is about to go downhill. A DEA lady is trying to save y'all but it's only so much I can do for you because Kane is a valuable informant."

"This is too much, Elina. How do I know you're telling the truth?" He asked as Elina went into a black on black truck and grabbed a thick folder for him.

"When you're done reading this file, you have to burn it, Sosa or I'll get in trouble"

"Why are you telling me all of this?"

"I don't know. Maybe, because I see a lot of good in you."

"Are the feds going to snatch my crew?" Sosa asked.

"The only people we really want are Barry, Wayne, and your mother. Sosa, I'm sorry but when you read the file, you will understand why. Your gang is being looked at, but we don't have no solid connection. We only have a few photos of you and Barry but I explained y'all just go out to eat. There is a lot of wiretaps of Barry talking about killing you and Kane and then using both crews to work from him.

"This is crazy."

"I know but Sosa you have to find a new plug because we got cameras and heavy wiretaps on Barry. You can get jammed up and bring your whole team down if you do anymore drug transactions with him," she stated.

"Aight thanks, Elina."

"I'll see you around. Be safe but most of all, smart," she said before getting in her truck.

Sosa rushed upstairs, feeling like a thousand pounds was on his shoulders. He couldn't believe what Elina told him.

He still had two hours and a half before Allure's flight landed. He had to read the file to see what the fuck was going on. The first person he saw was his mom's photo from two decades ago and she was pretty. Sosa read how his mom killed Barry's parents after he robbed her. It also said Barry had other kids on her. When it said his mom used to supply Barry, he was shocked. It said his mom had a Colombian connect, and they fell in love and ran off to down south.

Years later, the plug was murdered, and his mom went crazy. She wasn't the same since someone killed the plug, who was her lover.

Sosa couldn't believe his mom was a plug and was accused of thirty two murders in the Tri-State area from New York to Philly.

Wayne's photo was next. The feds wanted him because he killed a federal judge's son one morning in front of a IHOP restaurant. He was always on their radar for crimes that he did for Kane while he was in jail sending hits.

Barry's file was mainly that he was wanted for killing two cops, robbing a few dirty cops and extorting them. He was refusing to snitch, and masterminded seventeen murders in Philly within thirty years.

Sosa saw a few photos of him but nothing serious. His crew was straight but he could tell the feds also wanted Kane and why. They wanted another member of the Outlaws but they had no face or name for him. They had the Big Dawg written for the no photo man.

Sosa would've never thought Elina out of all people would be a fed. He wondered if he should warn his dad but then Sosa thought about how Elina told him Barry was trying get him out the way.

***

SOUTH PHILLY

Lez and Twin went out to a strip club with half of South Philly, having a good time but Lez just needed to clear his mind.

"That broad saved my life, bro," Lez said, thinking on how Janasia killed Tahiry a few days ago.

"You feeling shawty? Twin said, reading between the lines because he'd been talking about Janasia since they walked into the club.

"Why you say that?"

"Come on, cuz. It's cool and shit, but she still a cop. Well, DEA"

"She also a female too."

"So, get her on the team"

"To be real, I think she already on the team," Lez said, seeing a text from Sosa. Twin got a text from Sosa at the same time.

"Tomorrow night?" Lez asked reading the text.

"Yeah, he wants everybody there except Wayne," Twin said, wondering what was going down now.

CHAPTER 43
SPRINGFIELD, PHILLY

Elina waited for her number one rat. She recently recruited him after he got caught with sixty seven keys and two assault rifles in his car last month.

Elina's real name was Maura, but she used Elina at work. She was assigned to one of the biggest cases the city ever saw. Even bigger than the Black Mafia, Junior Mafia, and the Southside Crew.

Her career depended on this case, and she did everything correct, telling Sosa everything about the secret operation.

Telling Sosa was taking a big risk because he was about to make shit a lot easier or harder.

A BMW pulled up in front of the mansion, which was for sale but Elina was using the crib for secret meetings.

"Come to the back," she told her rat as they walked to the back near the two pools.

"Nice house, this yours?" Gee said, looking at her phat ass in the jeans.

"What you got for me?" She asked, seeing his eyes wonder on her body.

"Kane and Max having a private meeting later, but I wasn't invited. Foxy upset about her little shooter getting smoked by that DEA chick. She talking about killing the DEA chick because she shouldn't have been there," Gee stated every word he heard from Foxy two days ago when he went to cop some pounds of weed for his own personal use.

"When will you be ready to reup?" She asked, trying to get straight to business.

"Everything is dead right now Foxy told me"

"What? When did this fucking shit happen? That's the only reason why you're out!" She shouted.

"Foxy just told me. I don't know what's going on. Maybe it's a drought but I know in a few they going to drop me off a load. I paid them with the money for the keys y'all took from me so my order is in. Trust me, I got this," Gee stated.

"You got five days to have some shit recorded on that earring recorder or you going back to jail, but this time for a long time." She stormed off.

Gee shook his head, pissed off that he got himself into this crazy shit. He wished he would have stayed on the right path, doing the construction job, because his girlfriend, Latifah would have still been alive. Plus, he wouldn't be telling on the gang now.

Gee walked back to his BMW, seeing a familiar car drive down the suburb block. The white Jaguar window rolled, and Foxy smiled at him. She was with a Spanish chick.

"What's up bro? What you doing out here?" Foxy asked.

"I'm just house hunting. I want to get me a spot out here. What you doing out here?" Gee wanted to know because the area was a rich community.

"If you can afford some fly shit like this, I need to come work for you." Foxy joked.

"Shit me too," Shara said from the driver seat, looking cute with her hair and makeup done.

"Check it, I'm glad you here because a nigga, who live down the block, owe my dad a honey bun. I'm about to get it. Hop in," she told him.

"My car right there." Gee tried to talk his way out of it.

"It's straight. You coming right back," says Foxy.

They drove down the block and parked at a brickhouse before getting out. Gee followed their lead, forgetting he left his gun in the BMW. He would beat the shit out of the nigga, whoever he was, if he ain't want to pay Foxy. She knocked twice.

"We got to go through the back," Foxy said as she walked through the side of the house.

"You sure this nigga home? The house look empty," Gee said.

"Yeah, they here. Calm down, you know how old people be deaf," Foxy said now in the back.

210

"True." Gee looked into the backyard, realizing the place looked abandoned. Before he was about to say something, Foxy and Shara both pulled out guns.

"You thought we ain't know, nigga. Who you working for?" Foxy asked.

"Foxy, you bugging. I ain't no rat." Gee put his hands up.

"Nigga, the money you gave us was marked money, you dummy!" Foxy yelled.

"By Allah, I ain't tell nothing. Foxy please."

Boc... Boc... Boc... Boc... Boc...

"My bad, Shara," Foxy said to her new recruit who was supposed to shoot Gee first but she must have not upped.

"For what?" Shara said before Foxy blew her face off. Foxy left both of them dead in the backyard of a home that had been foreclosed for five years. Last night, she spoke to Max about the marked money. They all knew Gee was about to turn state, if he ain't already. So, she handled it. Rizzy wanted to but she thought it would be smarter if she did it. Gee wouldn't see it coming.

Foxy got in the truck and drove off, calling her dad turning down the Lil Durk music. She loved her some Lil Durk. She wanted a street nigga just like him.

"I took care of that," she said when he picked up.

"Alright, get rid of that car and the money."

"Okay."

"I'ma go to New York for a few days. I'll call you when I get back."

"What's up there?" She asked, but before he replied, there was a dial tone on the other end.

Foxy shook her head, turning up the music feeling like Kane had a second life or some shit. She ain't like the sneaky shit.

She drove back to West Philly, thinking about that DEA chick who shot her homegirl. Foxy wanted blood for that. She knew Lez would be coming for her, thinking she sent the hit but she didn't.

CHAPTER 44
ATLANTIC CITY, NJ

Sosa rented out a Rolls Royce limousine for the guys to take this trip to AC. Everybody was there. Lez, Lil Hak, Twin, and Lil Jet, who left Beth home to take care of his Jr. Wayne even came out and he hated partying.

The gang were all wearing white designer suits and looking like young bosses.

"My niggas, we really made it but now that we're elevating in the game, more problems are raising. Some serious shit has been brought to my attention," Sosa said.

"What you talking about?" Lez asked.

"Yeah, I thought shit was good?" Twin said as the limousine got off the highway.

"My father been with a woman named Elina for a little while now—"

"Man, get to the point," Lil Hak shouted, hating when Sosa told a whole movie just to get a point across.

"I am. Elina is a lawyer. We got close. Too close but she recently told me that she was a fed and was building a case on my dad," Sosa says.

"That mean they on to us?" Lil Jet asked.

"No, but they do have us on their radar, but they really want my dad and mom," Sosa told the crew.

"Your mom?" Twin asked.

"Come to find out, she was a plug and playing crazy all these years for a reason. The feds was watching her. I also believe they on Kane line because he a rat." Sosa saw a few faces light up except Wayne, who looked like it was nothing new.

"Hold on, bull. So we beefing with a rat?" Lil Jet asked.

"Yes," Wayne spoke up.

"You know?" Lez asked.

"Yes. I used to work for him while he was in jail, and he set me up. I ended up catching a few bodies and come to find out, he paid some niggas to get at me. He already knew the outcome. When I saw the statements, I couldn't believe it, but I realized he was trying to get out of jail," Wayne told them as some people gave off funny looks. They were not feeling him holding shit back.

"What a time to tell us," Lil Hak said taking a sip of Henny.

"We need to move smarter," Lez said thinking about what he was hearing, knowing Kane's beef could be their downfall. He wondered if Foxy knew her dad was a rat.

"Lez, the DEA chick is saving us but there is only so much she can do with the feds in town," Sosa said.

"She like him," Lil Jet said looking at Lez.

"Nigga shut up." Lez laughed.

"We need her to keep doing what she doing because the next few months going to get nasty," Sosa told them.

"I'ma take care of Max as soon as we get back. I think I can get a drop on him," Lil Hak stated.

"We need Rizzy and Foxy out the way," Twin stated.

"They found Gee dead last night in Springfield. So, that's one less problem," Sosa stated

"I can't believe he crossed us like that because I killed his sister by accident," Twin said.

"Fuck him. Let's enjoy this night," Sosa said grabbing a bottle of Cristal. The gang enjoyed the weekend in AC, living life and balling hard. They all blew over $40,000 apiece. Wayne and Lez lost over a hundred K.

***

Vera came out to a Dunkin Donuts to see her ex-husband. Their marriage was short lived because they both were still very young teenagers.

She had been keeping her distance from Kane lately because Vera knew he killed her son. She did her best at keeping Prince a secret, so for Kane to find out, meant he knew a lot more. Vera had her son, Prince with her ex-husband when they were creeping around while Kane was in prison.

She knew it was wrong to go back to her ex, but Vera needed comfort and he provided it at the time. Kane didn't even know about her marriage that lasted only a few months.

There were a few people inside Dunkin Donuts and her ex-husband was right in the back smiling. She hated his evil grins.

"Hey." She sat down, looking at Barry's calm, relaxed, demeanor.

"How you been, Vera?"

"Your son was killed."

"I know and I'm sorry for your grief," Barry stated.

"Our grief, asshole."

"My whole life is grief, Vera. I can't feel pain no more."

"If you knew he was killed, how come you ain't come to the funeral?"

"Just because you didn't see me, don't mean I wasn't there, Vera."

"If you say so, Barry. I just came to inform you because you're still his dad, no matter how much of a father you wasn't," she said, letting him know he was a deadbeat.

"You forced me to keep distance so you can keep him a secret. Do you not remember, Vera?"

"I ain't come here to go back and forth with you at all. So, I'ma leave. See you around." She got up.

"Do you know who did it?" Barry really wanted to know who killed his son just in case it was to target him.

"What does it matter to you?"

"I'm his father."

"That don't even sound right coming out our mouth, papi but you really want to know?" She asked.

"Yes."

"Kane," she said before walking out of the fast-food spot.

Barry couldn't believe his ears at all. He knew Kane and Vera were together but how could she let him kill their son. It didn't make any sense to him as he tried to put the pieces together. He wasn't a good dad to Prince because he played the background as Vera asked before Prince was born.

***

UPTOWN PHILLY

Zarhya survived the vicious pistol whipping, thanks to her friend Erica, who got the police there on time. One minute later, the doctors said she would have died if Erica ain't think fast and got help.

The damage was real. She had a broken nose, broken eye socket, and a cracked skull that almost took her out.

Sosa came by her apartment that he got her last week, so she could come home to her own crib. Today will be his first time asking her what happened because Zarhya ain't even tell the police what happened. She claimed she forgot but he knew that was a lie.

"You straight?" Sosa said, seeing his sister laid up in her bed.

"Thanks for the apartment and everything. It's real cozy," she said in her low pitch voice because it was hard to talk loud.

"I withdrew you from college but don't let this shit push you back from achieving your dreams." Sosa sat on the bed.

"I won't. I just need time to heal mentally, physically, and emotionally," she said.

Sosa tried not to look at her swollen face, but it was hard. It looked like a balloon.

"I understand and I want you to know that I'm here for you."

"Why you ain't come to the hospital?" She asked.

"When I went, I couldn't go inside. Shit, I tried not to think or talk about it, Zarhya."

"It wasn't your fault."

"I hope it wasn't but deep down I know it was. You ain't even have to tell me, sis. I know my lifestyle can have a bad effect on the people close to me," he told her.

"I made a bad choice."

"You?"

"Yes, my boyfriend Rizzy–"

"Rizzy?" Sosa said.

"Yes, he came by and just started to beat on me." She had tears in her eyes.

Sosa couldn't believe she was in a relationship with an opp. He blamed himself for not being more active in his sister's life because he could have saved her. He was glad she was still alive.

"It's okay."

"I love you," Zarhya said before she just stopped talking, wanting to get some sleep. Sosa stayed a few hours and was cursing himself for letting Rizzy get close to his family.

CHAPTER 45
YATTON, PHILLY

Max pulled into the rental car business establishment to change his Range Rover Evoque for something else. Every Friday, he switched cars just so the opps couldn't figure out what he was constantly driving.

Shit been so crazy. Staying felt like a struggle every day. The money wasn't worth the hurt and pain of losing friends and family. Being shot at everyday was starting to weigh real heavy on his heart.

Max rocked a Dior sweatsuit with a Ademar Piguet big face watch, walking inside with the car keys.

"I want that Audi A7 with the tint in the back," Max told the tall lanky worker behind the desk with glasses.

"Excuse me?"

"Nigga take these keys and here is 1000 dollars for the Audi out back next to the Lincoln," Max said placing the car key and money on the counter.

"I'ma need your ID to process the transaction," the man said.

"Here, and hurry up."

"Yes sir."

Max texted his new girl that he bagged in Atlanta last week when he went down there with Rizzy to fuck with some bitches.

Max really wanted to fuck Foxy because she was a bad gangster bitch. He knew her pussy had to be the bomb just by the way she carried herself. He knew those types of chicks had good pussy but were crazy if dicked down right.

"Sir, it says the last two cars you brought back had bullet holes in the door panels."

"Did I ask you that?"

"No, but I can't give you another car, sir."

"Listen here, you little bitch. You going to sign that form and I'ma walk out of her with the same car and we going to leave it at that." Max scared the hell out of him.

"Okay, Okay."

"And hurry the fuck up before I get mad in this bitch, bull!" Max shouted, seeing the man type into the computer."

"What's up, cuz?" Max answered Rizzy's call and placed in his earpiece.

"Where you at?" Rizzy asked.

"In Yatton."

"What the fuck you doing out there, my nigga?"

"I'm at the rental spot waiting on this clown ass nigga to finish this paperwork and he needs to hurry the fuck up," Max said loud enough so the tall kid could hear him. He worked as fast as he could to put Max in the system so he can get the fuck out of there.

"I need to see you, bro. I'm low and I got a move for twenty joints," Rizzy said.

"Where you at?"

"Coming from Delaware."

"Aight. By the time you touch down, I'll be ready for you, bull."

"Bet," Rizzy replied before hanging up.

Max was about wild out on the employee for taking so long until he saw him with a frightened look on his face.

Before looking behind him and out of the window, Max saw two black trucks pull up in the reflection of a mirror on the wall.

Tat... Tat... Tat... Tat... Tat... Tat... Tat... Tat... Tat... Tat... Tat... Tat...

Lil Hak and a gang of young bulls entered the store to see Max crawling on the floor with a gunshot wound to his back.

"I got him ... you get up out of here." Lil Hak told the employee who was ducked behind the counter, peeping his head up, before he ran out the back.

"Shit..." Max cried in pain from being shot in the lower back. The pain was going through his whole body like an electric shock.

"Outlaw, nigga!" Max spat while laid out on the floor.

"Y'all hear this nigga. On his last breath, he repping his gang. Now, that's loyalty," Lil Hak said before firing six shots in Max's face.

The gang hopped back in the trucks, sliding off. They were up on the scoreboard.

***

BENIHANA RESTAURANT, PHILLY

Sosa and Allure went out to eat so they could catch up on some missed time. Allure had been traveling a lot lately, modeling coast to coast.

"You look sexy tonight," she said.

"Thanks. I get clean from time to time but I missed you. Facetime all day ain't got shit on up close and personal."

"Facts. I feel the same, but my mom wants to meet you."

"Oh yeah?"

"Yeah, but right now, me and her got a little beef. She did some crazy shit that I didn't respect." Allure sounded disappointed.

"You want to talk about it?" Sosa knew there was something bothering Allure because her energy was off.

"Well, it's hard to explain." Allure ate her food.

"I'm listening."

"Okay, so my mom had another son but me and him didn't really have a relationship at all. He was in high school in York. He was a star basketball player, who got killed in his high school parking lot," Allure stated.

"Damn, I'm sorry, Allure." Sosa was speechless.

"It's cool. We really didn't have no bond, you know." Allure paused a moment as memories of that day flashed in her mind. "It's life but I felt like it was my fault because it was my beef."

"Don't blame yourself, Sosa. Shit happens in life. It's only going to make her stronger."

"I hope so, but no woman deserves to be abused in any way. I hate that," he said as she nodded. They enjoyed their dinner and went to take a walk at the waterfront, holding hands.

CHAPTER 46
DOWNTOWN PHILLY

The courthouse was packed at noon today and Janasia wanted nothing but to enjoy her lunch break as she walked through the crowd of people to exit the courthouse.

She been flooded with new cases, but one really caught her attention. A kid named Gee, who was found dead in the back of a home in the suburbs.

Walking outside with her briefcase, she wondered where she wanted to go eat. As Janasia approached her car, she saw a rose and a note on the windshield. It was classic attention snatcher. Janasia couldn't help but smile, picking up the small note that read 12pm Fogo De Choo beautiful Lez …

Staring into the sky, she realized how much of a gentleman he was. She hopped in her car and went to the Fogo De Choo Restaurant nearby for the lunch date as all types of thoughts filled up in her head.

When arriving at the restaurant, she saw Lez waiting out front and on his phone. At first, she wondered who he was talking to. Her purse had her work pistol inside so if he tried anything she would fry his ass in public.

"I thought you ain't talk to police." She approached him, smiling, seeing him hang up his iPhone.

"You're DEA, not a cop. You're worse," he joked.

"Whatever, but thanks for the rose. It was nice, and I really needed that."

"You're a queen. You shouldn't get nothing less but let's have lunch," Lez told her, opening the door for her. Janasia couldn't believe the chills she got around him.

Once seated, they chopped it up. Janasia had something she felt was bothering her.

"Can I trust you, Lez?"

"Trust me?" Yes, but let me tell you this. I will never fold, turn state, or violate my honor."

"Is that a yes, or no?" She ain't want to hear all that street talk. She heard it too many times until niggas started hearing double digits numbers.

"Yes."

"A man named Gee was recently murdered and a snitch is trying to frame your ex, Foxy," Janasia says.

"How do you know that's my ex?"

"I know a lot but anyway, it's a lot of snake shit going on within the Outlaws. Soon, the person trying to frame her will be trying to take you down. I just wanted to give you a heads up," she told him.

"Who is the person?"

"The crazy shit is it's her own father, Kane. He is trying to frame her on the body he turned in a truck and wiretaps because Gee started working with the feds. That's another thing. The feds are in town and a woman is trying to nail some big boys."

"I heard," Lez said.

"So, why are you still in the street? Look, I want to help you. Lez, I don't want to see you go down, so I've been trying to save you and your crew, but shit is getting tense."

"I know and thank you for everything, Janasia but I have to go."

"We ain't even eat yet."

"I'm sorry. I got to handle something," Lez stood up and leaned in, kissing her on the lips and she didn't resist.

"Uhmmmmm," she moaned, opening her eyes to see he was gone. That kiss touched her soul. She never felt something so special. Janasia hoped Lez would be smarter than the rest of his gang.

Janasia felt by telling him the info that he would fall back and take himself away from the bullshit going on. Her pussy was so creamy. She started to imagine what his dick game was like if that one kiss had her gushy.

***

PHILADELPHIA INTERNATIONAL AIRPORT, PHILLY
HOURS LATER

Lez had to reach out to Foxy on her Facebook and tell her it was important, and he needed to meet her ASAP. Foxy gave him the airport location.

Lez felt like if he told Foxy about her dad, then maybe she would slow down. Lez ain't wish jail on his worst enemy and deep down, he still cared for Foxy.

A Benz coupe pulled through the car lot speeding as he saw a plane take off.

Foxy hopped out with a Draco in her hand, but Lez stood in front of his car, knowing he would have been shot if she wanted him dead.

"I should kill you right now, nigga," Foxy said.

"Foxy, I called to save your life."

"Save me." She laughed, then got serious.

"Look, the feds are on you and Kane is working for them, trying to take you down. He ratted on Wayne too. That's how he got out of jail."

"Nigga, I should blow your fucking brains out for disrespecting me and my pops, nigga." She was mad.

"He's telling on how you killed Gee. He got the truck you used. He's working with feds. A DEA lady told me."

Foxy knew there had to be some truth to it because her dad was the only person who knew she killed Gee and used a truck to slide in. Kane also told her where to hide the truck. She gave Kane the murder weapon so he could get rid of it, but he was thirsty for the gun. Foxy started thinking back to other events that made her think Kane was moving real snake like.

"Fuck ..." she shouted.

"Be smart, Foxy. He dangerous. Save yourself," Lez told her.

"This shit is all because of y'all niggas!" She yelled.

"I ain't know you was in this shit, Foxy and on the opposite side. Come on, we go way back," Lez said as a Lexus creeped up from behind them and opened fire on them both.

Tat... Tat... Tat... Tat... Tat... Tat...

Foxy got hit twice and Lez once in his shoulder before shooting back and trying to save Foxy at the same time. When he saw Sosa firing, he almost dropped his gun as bullets continued to fly.

Tat... Tat... Tat... Tat... Tat... Tat... Tat... Tat...

The Lexus raced off as the airport cops came from the Gate 4 area rushing to the gunfire. Lez took Foxy's Draco, tossing it in his car as she was still breathing. He helped save her life until the EMT came.

CHAPTER 47
SOUTH PHILLY

Sosa drove into 5th Street Projects to pick up Lil Jet, who was awaiting him so they can go on their mission but Sosa couldn't believe what he just witnessed.

Allure needed a ride to the airport and Sosa took her so she could catch her flight to Atlanta for a photoshoot. Before he left the airport, he couldn't believe his eyes when he saw Lez talking to Foxy on some snake shit.

Sosa felt betrayal from his friend so he decided to make a move that would change everything with them. He knew about Lez and Foxy's relationship in the past, but shit was real in the streets right now. He ain't know who to trust.

If Sosa had to doubt one of his man's loyalty or trust, then he didn't need them around him. Making choice to shoot at both of them is something he was willing to live with and deal with whatever comes after.

Lil Jet was on the block with a few killers when Sosa pulled up, rolling down his window.

"You ready?" Sosa asked Lil Jet, who hopped off of the stairs.

"Yeah." Lil Jet shared some words with his young bulls, who were block huggers.

"Shit about to go sideways soon," Sosa told him when he pulled off onto the dark, scary Philly streets.

"What you mean?"

"I saw Lez and Foxy meeting up at the airport on some sneaking shit so I sent shots at both of them a few minutes ago." Sosa made a left at the end of the block, seeing police harass niggas on his right.

"What?" Lil Jet couldn't believe it.

"Yeah bro, I think he was about to cross us so I made the first move, bull. I ain't finna let him fuck us over," Sosa explained.

"He dead?"

"Nah, so we need to be a step ahead," Sosa stated.

"I think you should have at least asked Lez what happened before sliding on the bro. He still Sosa Gang." Lil Jet made sense and Sosa felt the same way.

"I know but it looked too shady and I ain't want to take no chances," Sosa says, feeling a little bad for not thinking shit out.

"That was a bad call but I'm with you. There is no turning back now, cuz."

"I know," Sosa added, driving towards uptown.

***

CLUB ACES, PHILLY

Wayne and a few of his boys were in the club having a ball. They were buying up all the expensive liquor and fucking with the baddest bitches in the club.

Tonight, was Wayne's birthday and he just wanted to drink and wash his pain away with the liquor.

Roddy's funeral was a mess. Never could he imagine someone really shooting up a church on some mad man, movie type shit.

Wayne hadn't been the same since Roddy's death. He didn't care about life itself no more. He ain't even want to sell drugs no more. The only thing on Wayne's mind was kill.

While in prison, he told himself that he would never go back to feeling like this and now he was back at square one.

"I'ma be back," Wayne told everybody.

"Where you going? " A sexy, thick, dark skinned chick with green eye contacts asked, trying to leave with Wayne tonight.

"To take a fucking piss. I'll be back in a second." Wayne walked out of the booth. He was a little tipsy making his way through the crowds of people.

Wayne hated being in tight spaces like clubs, especially dark spots. He had been in and out of jail his whole life, so he still had a prison mindset.

Luckily , the mens bathroom was empty. He rushed inside to take a urine because the liquor was running through his liver.

As he took a piss, he didn't see the two men dressed in black hoodies inside of a club, sneak inside.

A swing to his back made him jump back but that didn't stop the blows. Both had knives in their hands as they attacked Wayne, stabbing him in his neck, chest, heart, and organs repeatedly.

A dude walked into the restroom, seeing what was taking place and left scared to death.

Wayne's body was tossed in the toilet stall after he was stabbed over eighty two times.

Sosa and Lil Jet walked out of the club like it was nothing, exiting with their hoodies on.

Outside, they got in the car but as they were about to pull off, five D.C. Crew niggas saw them get in the car and opened fire on them.

The person who ran with them went to tell them two dudes were in the restroom stabbing Wayne up.

"Oh shit." Lil Jet ducked the bullets closing the car door as Sosa burned rubber, getting the fuck from out of there.

Sosa thought it would be good and quiet to bring knives in the club, so they didn't have to make too much noise. The gang made an agreement to kill Wayne because he was all for himself and his crew. To only make shit worse, the feds wanted him and the gang ain't need that attention.

"You think them niggas knew it was us?" Lil Jet asked.

"Fuck it, if they do," Sosa stated knowing more problems were about to follow up after Wayne's death.

***

NICETOWN, PHILLY
ONE MONTH LATER

OG Kane, Foxy and Rizzy all attended the meeting in a building Kane rented out for the day.

"Today is a big day because as you know, there is two more Outlaw leading members that the both of you never met but today you will. We lost Gee and Max and that's a part of the game.

I ain't lose no sleep but it's time we elevate," Kane said.

"What happen to Sosa Gang?" Rizzy asked.

"Fuck 'em. They can't stop us, Rizzy. We locking the streets down and our crew is growing every day. Special thanks to my lovely daughter and you." Kane saw Foxy fake smile.

"Before I bring out the two leaders, I have a special guest," Kane said as he yelled for two men to bring out the surprise.

There was a wheelchair and a man with black pillowcase over his head was seated in it. The two men left the wheelchair there and walked off.

"Who dat?" Foxy asked.

"One less problem," Kane got up and snatched the pillowcase off the man's head.

Twin's face was bloody with duct tape covering his mouth. Kane caught Twin slipping two nights ago and had his goon kidnap him.

"Ain't this some shit?" Rizzy clutched his weapon.

"I'ma bringing out our guests. First person, come out," Kane said as Foxy and Rizzy broke their necks to see who else had a seat at the table.

Janasia walked out in a suit and the look on Foxy's face said it all. She knew who the woman was.

"She DEA," Foxy said

"Yes, but she is also a leading member for over ten years. Her father basically started the Outlaws with the help of the next man, who is also my plug," Kane said as his next guest walked out.

A tall man with a Muslim beard came out wearing a garment and giving Janasia a hug. He hadn't seen her in years because they both played the background. They let the other members run the show, but it was time they stepped in.

When Twin saw the man with the beard, he couldn't believe it as he been listening to every word.

Twin's heart almost dropped as he looked at his father, Imam Ahmad.

"They had been running the show from behind the scenes for years, especially Ahmad.

"It's nice to meet y'all, Foxy and Rizzy, but starting today new rules will be placed and things will change," Imam Ahmad said, seeing an awkward look on all of their faces.

"This is very past due," Janasia said as her and Imam Ahmad pulled out guns.

Boc... Boc... Boc... Boc... Boc... Boc... Boc... Boc...

They aired Kane's body out with bullets before two men ran in the room to remove Kane's dead body. Foxy and Rizzy couldn't believe what just went down so fast.

"Do you have a problem with us killing your rat ass father?" Janasia asked Foxy as she saw her look as if Foxy wanted to try something.

"Not at all," Foxy replied.

"Good. Now, let's get down to business and get to a bag," Janasia said.

"First off, let me start by saying this is my son right here," Imam Ahmad said cutting off Twin's wrist and ankle tapes. Then, removing his tape on his face.

Foxy and Rizzy couldn't adjust to everything they had been seeing in the last five minutes.

"Dad, what the fuck is going on?" Twin stood up.

"I'ma give you an option to either take Kane's position in the Outlaws or you can die with your friend. Twin, you have seventy-two hours to make your choice," Imam Ahmad said before four men escorted Twin out the building and letting him go free.

"I don't think that was smart to let him go," Rizzy said

"Did I ask you?" Imam Ahmad looked at Rizzy, who shut up.

"This is a new quarter, and we got some shit planned. We just have to clean up some loose ends," Janasia said ice grilling Foxy and peeping her dirty looks.

"There will be more bodies, more money, and more drama now. Be ready. We all family now, Janasia and Foxy," Imam Ahmad said before turning to leave.

Rizzy knew shit was about to get real spicy.

Foxy got up and left, thinking about how they just murked Kane right in front of her. She wanted to kill him herself, so she wasn't feeling how they did that in front of her. Janasia walked out laughing with Rizzy behind her, ready for this new chapter.

***

PHILLY, PA

Sosa ordered a private jet to take him to Miami so he could get away and spend some time alone at his condo that he copped.

Shit was getting odd. Everybody had been acting funny. Twin became nowhere to be found and Lez became a ghost. He just needed to clear his thoughts and reconnect with his inner self.

Sosa took a nap on the private jet. This was the first nap he took in almost two days.

***

Hours later, Sosa woke up realizing he had been asleep close to five hours and the jet was just landing. He knew it only took two hours the most to get to Miami on a plane and a jet was much faster.

Looking out the window Sosa saw all types of tropical trees and a different environment. Sosa knew he wasn't in Miami at all, especially when he saw six trucks pull up and surround the jet.

Sosa grabbed his gun and went to the pilot cabin but the door was locked and bulletproof.

"Fuck." Sosa knew it was a setup, so he figured why not go out with a bang. He opened the door and saw over twenty Spanish looking men waiting on him.

When he was about to start busting his Glock 22 with a thirty-two shot clip, he saw a pretty older woman get out of one of the trucks in a black dress. The closer she got, he was shocked to see it was his mom.

"We have to go, son. Welcome to Colombia. Come give mommy a hug," Sosa's mom said smiling as he got off the jet confused ...

TO BE CONTINUED...
SOSA GANG 3
COMING SOON

Lock Down Publications and Ca$h Presents assisted publishing packages.

BASIC PACKAGE $499
Editing
Cover Design
Formatting

UPGRADED PACKAGE $800
Typing
Editing
Cover Design
Formatting

ADVANCE PACKAGE $1,200
Typing
Editing
Cover Design
Formatting
Copyright registration
Proofreading
Upload book to Amazon

LDP SUPREME PACKAGE $1,500
Typing
Editing
Cover Design
Formatting
Copyright registration
Proofreading
Set up Amazon account
Upload book to Amazon
Advertise on LDP Amazon and Facebook page

***Other services available upon request. Additional charges may apply

Lock Down Publications
P.O. Box 944
Stockbridge, GA 30281-9998
Phone # 470 303-9761

Submission Guideline

Submit the first three chapters of your completed manuscript to ldpsubmissions@gmail.com, subject line: Your book's title. The manuscript must be in a .doc file and sent as an attachment. Document should be in Times New Roman, double spaced and in size 12 font. Also, provide your synopsis and full contact information. If sending multiple submissions, they must each be in a separate email.

Have a story but no way to send it electronically? You can still submit to LDP/Ca$h Presents. Send in the first three chapters, written or typed, of your completed manuscript to:

LDP: Submissions Dept
Po Box 944
Stockbridge, Ga 30281

DO NOT send original manuscript. Must be a duplicate.

Provide your synopsis and a cover letter containing your full contact information.

Thanks for considering LDP and Ca$h Presents.

<u>NEW RELEASES</u>

THE COCAINE PRINCESS 7 by KING RIO

GRIMEY WAYS 3 by RAY VINCI

HEAVEN GOT A GHETTO by RENTA

SOSA GANG 2 by ROMELL TUKES

Coming Soon from Lock Down Publications/Ca$h Presents

BLOOD OF A BOSS **VI**

SHADOWS OF THE GAME II

TRAP BASTARD II

By **Askari**

LOYAL TO THE GAME **IV**

By **T.J. & Jelissa**

TRUE SAVAGE **VIII**

MIDNIGHT CARTEL IV

DOPE BOY MAGIC IV

CITY OF KINGZ III

NIGHTMARE ON SILENT AVE II

THE PLUG OF LIL MEXICO II

CLASSIC CITY II

By **Chris Green**

BLAST FOR ME **III**

A SAVAGE DOPEBOY III

CUTTHROAT MAFIA III

DUFFLE BAG CARTEL VII

HEARTLESS GOON VI

By **Ghost**

A HUSTLER'S DECEIT III

KILL ZONE II

BAE BELONGS TO ME III

TIL DEATH II

By **Aryanna**

KING OF THE TRAP III

By **T.J. Edwards**

GORILLAZ IN THE BAY V

3X KRAZY III

Romell Tukes

STRAIGHT BEAST MODE III
De'Kari
KINGPIN KILLAZ IV
STREET KINGS III
PAID IN BLOOD III
CARTEL KILLAZ IV
DOPE GODS III
Hood Rich
SINS OF A HUSTLA II
ASAD
YAYO V
Bred In The Game 2
S. Allen
THE STREETS WILL TALK II
By Yolanda Moore
SON OF A DOPE FIEND III
HEAVEN GOT A GHETTO III
SKI MASK MONEY II
By Renta
LOYALTY AIN'T PROMISED III
By Keith Williams
I'M NOTHING WITHOUT HIS LOVE II
SINS OF A THUG II
TO THE THUG I LOVED BEFORE II
IN A HUSTLER I TRUST II
By Monet Dragun
QUIET MONEY IV
EXTENDED CLIP III
THUG LIFE IV
By Trai'Quan

THE STREETS MADE ME IV

By **Larry D. Wright**

IF YOU CROSS ME ONCE III

ANGEL V

By **Anthony Fields**

THE STREETS WILL NEVER CLOSE IV

By **K'ajji**

HARD AND RUTHLESS III

KILLA KOUNTY IV

By **Khufu**

MONEY GAME III

By **Smoove Dolla**

JACK BOYS VS DOPE BOYS IV

A GANGSTA'S QUR'AN V

COKE GIRLZ II

COKE BOYS II

LIFE OF A SAVAGE V

CHI'RAQ GANGSTAS V

SOSA GANG III

BRONX SAVAGES II

BODYMORE KINGPINS II

By **Romell Tukes**

MURDA WAS THE CASE III

Elijah R. Freeman

AN UNFORESEEN LOVE IV

BABY, I'M WINTERTIME COLD III

By **Meesha**

QUEEN OF THE ZOO III

By **Black Migo**

CONFESSIONS OF A JACKBOY III

By Nicholas Lock

KING KILLA II

By Vincent "Vitto" Holloway

BETRAYAL OF A THUG III

By Fre$h

THE MURDER QUEENS III

By Michael Gallon

THE BIRTH OF A GANGSTER III

By Delmont Player

TREAL LOVE II

By Le'Monica Jackson

FOR THE LOVE OF BLOOD III

By Jamel Mitchell

RAN OFF ON DA PLUG II

By Paper Boi Rari

HOOD CONSIGLIERE III

By Keese

PRETTY GIRLS DO NASTY THINGS II

By Nicole Goosby

PROTÉGÉ OF A LEGEND III

LOVE IN THE TRENCHES II

By Corey Robinson

IT'S JUST ME AND YOU II

By Ah'Million

BORN IN THE GRAVE III

By Self Made Tay

FOREVER GANGSTA III

By Adrian Dulan

GORILLAZ IN THE TRENCHES II

Sosa Gang 2

By SayNoMore

THE COCAINE PRINCESS VIII

By King Rio

CRIME BOSS II

Playa Ray

LOYALTY IS EVERYTHING III

Molotti

HERE TODAY GONE TOMORROW II

By Fly Rock

REAL G'S MOVE IN SILENCE II

By Von Diesel

GRIMEY WAYS IV

By Ray Vinci

Available Now

RESTRAINING ORDER **I & II**

By **CA$H & Coffee**

LOVE KNOWS NO BOUNDARIES **I II & III**

By **Coffee**

RAISED AS A GOON I, II, III & IV

BRED BY THE SLUMS I, II, III

BLAST FOR ME I & II

ROTTEN TO THE CORE I II III

A BRONX TALE I, II, III

DUFFLE BAG CARTEL I II III IV V VI

Romell Tukes

HEARTLESS GOON I II III IV V

A SAVAGE DOPEBOY I II

DRUG LORDS I II III

CUTTHROAT MAFIA I II

KING OF THE TRENCHES

By **Ghost**

LAY IT DOWN **I & II**

LAST OF A DYING BREED I II

BLOOD STAINS OF A SHOTTA I & II III

By **Jamaica**

LOYAL TO THE GAME I II III

LIFE OF SIN I, II III

By **TJ & Jelissa**

BLOODY COMMAS I & II

SKI MASK CARTEL I II & III

KING OF NEW YORK I II,III IV V

RISE TO POWER I II III

COKE KINGS I II III IV V

BORN HEARTLESS I II III IV

KING OF THE TRAP I II

By **T.J. Edwards**

IF LOVING HIM IS WRONG…I & II

LOVE ME EVEN WHEN IT HURTS I II III

By **Jelissa**

WHEN THE STREETS CLAP BACK I & II III

THE HEART OF A SAVAGE I II III IV

MONEY MAFIA I II

LOYAL TO THE SOIL I II III

By **Jibril Williams**

A DISTINGUISHED THUG STOLE MY HEART I II & III

242

LOVE SHOULDN'T HURT I II III IV
RENEGADE BOYS I II III IV
PAID IN KARMA I II III
SAVAGE STORMS I II III
AN UNFORESEEN LOVE I II III
BABY, I'M WINTERTIME COLD I II
By **Meesha**
A GANGSTER'S CODE I &, II III
A GANGSTER'S SYN I II III
THE SAVAGE LIFE I II III
CHAINED TO THE STREETS I II III
BLOOD ON THE MONEY I II III
A GANGSTA'S PAIN I II III
By J-Blunt
PUSH IT TO THE LIMIT
By **Bre' Hayes**
BLOOD OF A BOSS **I, II, III, IV, V**
SHADOWS OF THE GAME
TRAP BASTARD
By **Askari**
THE STREETS BLEED MURDER **I, II & III**
THE HEART OF A GANGSTA I II& III
By **Jerry Jackson**
CUM FOR ME I II III IV V VI VII VIII
An **LDP Erotica Collaboration**
BRIDE OF A HUSTLA **I II & II**
THE FETTI GIRLS **I, II& III**
CORRUPTED BY A GANGSTA I, II III, IV
BLINDED BY HIS LOVE
THE PRICE YOU PAY FOR LOVE I, II ,III

DOPE GIRL MAGIC I II III
By **Destiny Skai**
WHEN A GOOD GIRL GOES BAD
By **Adrienne**
THE COST OF LOYALTY I II III
By Kweli
A GANGSTER'S REVENGE **I II III & IV**
THE BOSS MAN'S DAUGHTERS I II III IV V
A SAVAGE LOVE **I & II**
BAE BELONGS TO ME I II
A HUSTLER'S DECEIT I, II, III
WHAT BAD BITCHES DO I, II, III
SOUL OF A MONSTER I II III
KILL ZONE
A DOPE BOY'S QUEEN I II III
TIL DEATH
By **Aryanna**
A KINGPIN'S AMBITON
A KINGPIN'S AMBITION **II**
I MURDER FOR THE DOUGH
By **Ambitious**
TRUE SAVAGE I II III IV V VI VII
DOPE BOY MAGIC I, II, III
MIDNIGHT CARTEL I II III
CITY OF KINGZ I II
NIGHTMARE ON SILENT AVE
THE PLUG OF LIL MEXICO II
CLASSIC CITY
By **Chris Green**
A DOPEBOY'S PRAYER

Sosa Gang 2

By **Eddie "Wolf" Lee**
THE KING CARTEL **I, II & III**
By **Frank Gresham**
THESE NIGGAS AIN'T LOYAL **I, II & III**
By **Nikki Tee**
GANGSTA SHYT **I II &III**
By **CATO**
THE ULTIMATE BETRAYAL
By **Phoenix**
BOSS'N UP **I , II & III**
By **Royal Nicole**
I LOVE YOU TO DEATH
By **Destiny J**
I RIDE FOR MY HITTA
I STILL RIDE FOR MY HITTA
By **Misty Holt**
LOVE & CHASIN' PAPER
By **Qay Crockett**
TO DIE IN VAIN
SINS OF A HUSTLA
By **ASAD**
BROOKLYN HUSTLAZ
By **Boogsy Morina**
BROOKLYN ON LOCK I & II
By **Sonovia**
GANGSTA CITY
By **Teddy Duke**
A DRUG KING AND HIS DIAMOND I & II III
A DOPEMAN'S RICHES
HER MAN, MINE'S TOO I, II

Romell Tukes

CASH MONEY HO'S

THE WIFEY I USED TO BE I II

PRETTY GIRLS DO NASTY THINGS

By Nicole Goosby

TRAPHOUSE KING **I II & III**

KINGPIN KILLAZ I II III

STREET KINGS I II

PAID IN BLOOD **I II**

CARTEL KILLAZ I II III

DOPE GODS I II

By **Hood Rich**

LIPSTICK KILLAH **I, II, III**

CRIME OF PASSION I II & III

FRIEND OR FOE I II III

By **Mimi**

STEADY MOBBN' **I, II, III**

THE STREETS STAINED MY SOUL I II III

By **Marcellus Allen**

WHO SHOT YA **I, II, III**

SON OF A DOPE FIEND I II

HEAVEN GOT A GHETTO I II

SKI MASK MONEY

Renta

GORILLAZ IN THE BAY **I II III IV**

TEARS OF A GANGSTA I II

3X KRAZY I II

STRAIGHT BEAST MODE I II

DE'KARI

TRIGGADALE I II III

MURDAROBER WAS THE CASE I II

Elijah R. Freeman
GOD BLESS THE TRAPPERS I, II, III
THESE SCANDALOUS STREETS I, II, III
FEAR MY GANGSTA I, II, III IV, V
THESE STREETS DON'T LOVE NOBODY I, II
BURY ME A G I, II, III, IV, V
A GANGSTA'S EMPIRE I, II, III, IV
THE DOPEMAN'S BODYGAURD I II
THE REALEST KILLAZ I II III
THE LAST OF THE OGS I II III
Tranay Adams
THE STREETS ARE CALLING
Duquie Wilson
MARRIED TO A BOSS I II III
By Destiny Skai & Chris Green
KINGZ OF THE GAME I II III IV V VI
CRIME BOSS
Playa Ray
SLAUGHTER GANG I II III
RUTHLESS HEART I II III
By Willie Slaughter
FUK SHYT
By Blakk Diamond
DON'T F#CK WITH MY HEART I II
By Linnea
ADDICTED TO THE DRAMA I II III
IN THE ARM OF HIS BOSS II
By Jamila
YAYO I II III IV
A SHOOTER'S AMBITION I II

Romell Tukes

BRED IN THE GAME
By S. Allen
TRAP GOD I II III
RICH $AVAGE I II III
MONEY IN THE GRAVE I II III
By Martell Troublesome Bolden
FOREVER GANGSTA I II
GLOCKS ON SATIN SHEETS I II
By Adrian Dulan
TOE TAGZ I II III IV
LEVELS TO THIS SHYT I II
IT'S JUST ME AND YOU
By Ah'Million
KINGPIN DREAMS I II III
RAN OFF ON DA PLUG
By Paper Boi Rari
CONFESSIONS OF A GANGSTA I II III IV
CONFESSIONS OF A JACKBOY I II
By Nicholas Lock
I'M NOTHING WITHOUT HIS LOVE
SINS OF A THUG
TO THE THUG I LOVED BEFORE
A GANGSTA SAVED XMAS
IN A HUSTLER I TRUST
By Monet Dragun
CAUGHT UP IN THE LIFE I II III
THE STREETS NEVER LET GO I II III
By Robert Baptiste
NEW TO THE GAME I II III
MONEY, MURDER & MEMORIES I II III

248

Sosa Gang 2

By **Malik D. Rice**
LIFE OF A SAVAGE I II III IV
A GANGSTA'S QUR'AN I II III IV
MURDA SEASON I II III
GANGLAND CARTEL I II III
CHI'RAQ GANGSTAS I II III IV
KILLERS ON ELM STREET I II III
JACK BOYZ N DA BRONX I II III
A DOPEBOY'S DREAM I II III
JACK BOYS VS DOPE BOYS I II III
COKE GIRLZ
COKE BOYS
SOSA GANG I II
BRONX SAVAGES
BODYMORE KINGPINS
By **Romell Tukes**
LOYALTY AIN'T PROMISED I II
By **Keith Williams**
QUIET MONEY I II III
THUG LIFE I II III
EXTENDED CLIP I II
A GANGSTA'S PARADISE
By **Trai'Quan**
THE STREETS MADE ME I II III
By **Larry D. Wright**
THE ULTIMATE SACRIFICE I, II, III, IV, V, VI
KHADIFI
IF YOU CROSS ME ONCE I II
ANGEL I II III IV
IN THE BLINK OF AN EYE

Romell Tukes

By Anthony Fields

THE LIFE OF A HOOD STAR

By Ca$h & Rashia Wilson

THE STREETS WILL NEVER CLOSE I II III

By K'ajji

CREAM I II III

THE STREETS WILL TALK

By Yolanda Moore

NIGHTMARES OF A HUSTLA I II III

By King Dream

CONCRETE KILLA I II III

VICIOUS LOYALTY I II III

By Kingpen

HARD AND RUTHLESS I II

MOB TOWN 251

THE BILLIONAIRE BENTLEYS I II III

REAL G'S MOVE IN SILENCE

By Von Diesel

GHOST MOB

Stilloan Robinson

MOB TIES I II III IV V VI

SOUL OF A HUSTLER, HEART OF A KILLER I II

GORILLAZ IN THE TRENCHES

By SayNoMore

BODYMORE MURDERLAND I II III

THE BIRTH OF A GANGSTER I II

By Delmont Player

FOR THE LOVE OF A BOSS

By C. D. Blue

MOBBED UP I II III IV

THE BRICK MAN I II III IV V
THE COCAINE PRINCESS I II III IV V VI VII
By King Rio
KILLA KOUNTY I II III IV
By Khufu
MONEY GAME I II
By Smoove Dolla
A GANGSTA'S KARMA I II III
By FLAME
KING OF THE TRENCHES I II III
by **GHOST & TRANAY ADAMS**
QUEEN OF THE ZOO I II
By **Black Migo**
GRIMEY WAYS I II III
By Ray Vinci
XMAS WITH AN ATL SHOOTER
By Ca$h & Destiny Skai
KING KILLA
By Vincent "Vitto" Holloway
BETRAYAL OF A THUG I II
By Fre$h
THE MURDER QUEENS I II
By Michael Gallon
TREAL LOVE
By Le'Monica Jackson
FOR THE LOVE OF BLOOD I II
By Jamel Mitchell
HOOD CONSIGLIERE I II
By Keese
PROTÉGÉ OF A LEGEND I II

LOVE IN THE TRENCHES
By Corey Robinson
BORN IN THE GRAVE I II
By Self Made Tay
MOAN IN MY MOUTH
By XTASY
TORN BETWEEN A GANGSTER AND A GENTLEMAN
By J-BLUNT & Miss Kim
LOYALTY IS EVERYTHING I II
Molotti
HERE TODAY GONE TOMORROW
By Fly Rock
PILLOW PRINCESS
By S. Hawkins

BOOKS BY LDP'S CEO, CA$H

TRUST IN NO MAN

TRUST IN NO MAN 2

TRUST IN NO MAN 3

BONDED BY BLOOD

SHORTY GOT A THUG

THUGS CRY

THUGS CRY 2

THUGS CRY 3

TRUST NO BITCH

TRUST NO BITCH 2

TRUST NO BITCH 3

TIL MY CASKET DROPS

RESTRAINING ORDER

RESTRAINING ORDER 2

IN LOVE WITH A CONVICT

LIFE OF A HOOD STAR

XMAS WITH AN ATL SHOOTER

Romell Tukes

www.ingramcontent.com/pod-product-compliance
Lightning Source LLC
Chambersburg PA
CBHW071139260626
47162CB00003B/850